"Find pink slippers that fit," a young man told Joey, cocking his head toward a huge table that held satin slippers, feather boas, and various props. Joey found some pink slippers and changed into them. Then she stood on the porch, feeling like an idiot and an imposter, while the other models chatted easily with each other.

Renaldo walked over to them. He was naked except for a pair of cherry-red silk boxer shorts.

"Renaldo! I didn't know you were doing this shoot," Royce squealed, giving Renaldo a kiss.

"Please, I just redid your lips, no kissing!" someone instructed.

Véronique hurried over to them. "Where's A.P.?"

"There was some kind of mixup about which outfit was first, and he—" Renaldo began. "Oh, wait, here he comes."

The door to the guys' trailer swung open and another male model in a bathrobe stepped down.

Joey's jaw dropped open. Walking toward her looking beyond perfect, wearing a black silk robe and black silk pajama bottoms, was Aaron Poole, the model from her Advanced Life Drawing class.

DAWSON'S CREEK™

Don't miss any of these
Dawson's Creek™ books
featuring your favorite characters!

Dawson's Creek™ The Beginning of Everything Else
*A Novelization based on the hit television show
produced by Columbia TriStar Television.*

• Four new, original stories featuring your favorite characters
from *Dawson's Creek™*, the hit television show.

LONG HOT SUMMER
CALM BEFORE THE STORM
SHIFTING INTO OVERDRIVE
MAJOR MELTDOWN

And don't miss:

• **Dawson's Creek™** The Official Scrapbook

• **Dawson's Creek™** The Official Postcard Book

Available now from Pocket Books.

Check wherever books are available.

Visit Pocket Books on the World Wide Web
http://www.SimonSays.com

Visit the Sony website at
http://www.dawsonscreek.com

Dawson's Creek™

Double Exposure

Based on the television series "Dawson's Creek"™
created by **Kevin Williamson**

Written by C. J. Anders

POCKET BOOKS

New York   London   Toronto   Sydney   Tokyo   Singapore

This book is a work of fiction. Names, characters, places and incidents are products of the author's imagination or are used fictiously. Any resemblance to actual events or locales or persons living or dead is entirely coincidental.

An *Original* Publication of POCKET BOOKS

POCKET BOOKS, a division of Simon & Schuster Inc.
1230 Avenue of the Americas, New York, NY 10020

Copyright © 1999 by Columbia TriStar Television, Inc.
All Rights Reserved.

Front and back cover photographs copyright © 1999 by Columbia TriStar Television, Inc.
Front cover photographs by Mark Kayne

ISBN: 0-671-03526-6

First Pocket Books printing March 1999

10 9 8 7 6 5 4 3 2 1

POCKET and colophon are registered trademarks of Simon & Schuster Inc.

DAWSON'S CREEK is a registered trademark of Columbia TriStar Television, Inc.

Printed in the U.S.A.

For Maia, and with thanks to Jeff's parents, at whose country place in Stockbridge, Massachusetts, we wrote this novel

Chapter 1

"**W**elcome to the wonderful world of Advanced Life Drawing," Andie McPhee sang out to her friend Joey Potter as the two of them found seats in the art room.

Joey pulled her new sketch pad out of her backpack. "I ask you, Andie, what would anyone in this microscopic slice of adolescent angst known as Capeside High School know about drawing life? Being able to draw life sort of assumes that we actually *live* life, which we do not."

"Yes we do, in a limited, stereotypical, small New England coastal town sort of way," Andie said. "I find us very sweet."

"Swell." Joey pulled her hair back and refastened her scrunchie. "So, do you draw?"

"Let me put it to you this way. In fourth grade our teacher had us all draw pictures of springtime.

He said my drawing of a groundhog seeing his own shadow was so good, he put it up on the bulletin board."

"So you can draw," Joey surmised.

"Not exactly. It was supposed to be a self-portrait. You know, Andie frolicking in the spring rain, looking at her shadow in a puddle—that kind of thing. Needless to say, I took the A and kept my mouth shut."

"Well, I'd say that bodes well for you to ace Advanced Life Drawing." Joey rummaged through her backpack in search of the charcoal and art gum eraser she'd thrown in there that morning.

"I hope," Andie replied. "Actually, I didn't have much choice about this class. The computer messed up my schedule, so it was either Advanced Life Drawing, Introduction to Sports Coaching, or . . . Lust for Life."

Joey laughed. "Dream on. I know that charcoal is in here someplace. . . ."

"The movie, Joey, the movie," Andie explained. "*Lust for Life*? Young, studly Kirk Douglas as Vincent van Gogh? Look up."

Joey did.

Sitting on a stool at the front of the room was a guy who looked eerily like young Kirk Douglas, only hotter.

"I would have to say: Wow."

"My sentiments exactly," Andie agreed. "But unlike van Gogh, he appears to have two ears. Maybe you should get up close and personal so we'll know for sure."

"Thank you, but I'm sure my imagination can fill

in any anatomical parts that might be missing." She finally unearthed her charcoal. It was stuck to one of her nephew's pacifiers. "Oh, yuck."

Andie got a tissue out of her backpack and handed it to Joey, her eyes still on the guy across the room. "You think he's the life model?"

"No, I think he decided to wear that bathrobe as a fashion statement."

"That's more Pacey's style," Andie said dryly as she reached for a notebook. She opened it and began checking things off on a list. "Witter's Law #3: Why dress up when you'll just have to undress again at the end of the day?"

Joey opened her pad. "To know him is to love him."

"Unfortunately, I agree," Andie said.

Joey raised her eyebrows. "Unfortunately?"

"Pacey is . . . well, you know what Pacey is." She tapped her pen thoughtfully against her list. "Let's see, if I grocery shop right after school and the lines aren't too long, I can make something really easy for dinner, and then if I don't have more than an hour of bio homework, that'll still leave me enough time to get to the library for my research paper. Oh no, wait, I have to study for the history quiz, too." She added it to her list.

"Did you schedule in time to wash, brush your teeth, breathe, little things like that?" Joey asked.

"I've decided breathing is a self-indulgent waste of precious time," Andie said, still studying her list.

"I thought Pacey told me you two were going to the movies tonight."

"That was Plan A," Andie admitted, "but Plan A

died about eight o'clock last night, when we moved on to Plan B."

"Meaning?" Joey asked.

"Meaning he called, I cancelled." Andie threw her notebook into her backpack. "I don't have time to see a movie. Pacey wasn't exactly happy with me, either. Actually, we had what you could call a minor disagreement."

"How minor?"

Andie sighed. "On a seismic scale of one to ten, with ten being California falling into the ocean, I'd say we're talking a six-point-five."

Joey winced. "Ouch."

"I know," Andie agreed. "It's just that Pacey always wants to have fun. I don't have time for fun right now."

Joey nodded. She knew Andie's mom had serious emotional problems, which meant that when her mom went through a bad period, Andie had to pick up the slack at home. It wasn't fair any more than it was fair that her own mom was dead, but it was just the way it was.

"So," Andie went on, "the upshot of this little wrinkle in our relationship was that we—okay, I—sort of decided that we should both be free to see other people."

"Color me shocked," Joey said. "That's what you want?"

"Yes. No. Well, maybe," Andie said. "It just feels like as much as I'm into Pacey, I don't have time to be his girlfriend right now. At least not the kind of girlfriend Pacey wants me to be. Party hearty and all that."

"Oh, come on, Andie, he wants you more than he wants—"

"I break dates with him all the time lately," Andie said, her voice rising. "He's always saying 'relax, Andie, life is too short,' like he doesn't even get what I'm going through. It's just . . . it's more pressure than I can handle right now."

Andie's fight with Pacey kept playing over and over in her mind, like a tape on endless rewind. Thinking about it was even more exhausting than trying to be his girlfriend.

Andie checked her watch. "Mark Ms. Lewinger tardy. Let's talk about something less serious, okay? Like art."

"Art *is* serious," Joey said.

"For you. But, then, you have talent. No one would mistake your self-portrait for a groundhog."

Joey smiled. Joey Potter, Artist. She rolled the phrase around in her mind. Could a too tall, formerly awkward, still shy girl from the wrong side of the tracks find her true self as an artist?

That was exactly what seemed to be happening to her. So many people had encouraged her lately—even Professor Harris at the college art class she had taken—that she was kind of starting to believe it herself.

After all, if Dawson Leery, her best friend since forever, could find himself making films, why couldn't Joey Potter find herself making art? Dawson always said that if you had a passion for something, then . . .

She stopped her own mind from completing that thought. Why did she spend so much time thinking about what Dawson said, what Dawson thought, what Dawson did?

He isn't your boyfriend anymore, she reminded herself. And even if he were, it's not about him, it's about you. You deserve a passion that is yours alone, one that has nothing to do with Dawson Leery. Or any other guy, for that matter.

She'd told herself this many times before. Which was why it was so maddening that her mind drifted to him so often. Old habits just died hard.

"Students, your attention, please?"

Joey looked up. The principal's secretary stood in the doorway. "Ms. Lewinger has been detained," the secretary said. "She'll be here shortly. Please stay in your seats and talk quietly." She smiled and left.

Immediately a dozen kids left their seats and the room filled with loud, boisterous voices. Someone turned on a radio and rap music filled the air.

Joey closed her eyes. She was no longer at school. Instead, she was at the Boston Museum of Fine Arts. In her mind, she could visualize the incredible paintings by Romare Beardon she'd seen there a few months earlier. The exhibit had changed her life. Now, in her free time, she often found herself sketching. The more she drew, the more she loved it. That was the good part. The bad part was, the more she drew, the more critical she was of her own work. She had so much to learn.

"You have to admit, that guy gives new meaning to the word *fine*," Jen said.

Joey and Andie both craned their necks around. Jen was sitting on Tolliver Heath's desk, her chin in her hand, staring at the male model. Tolliver, a small, nerdy guy who was the best artist in the school, looked as if he had died and gone to heaven.

Jen Lindley was a gorgeous, curvy blonde who had moved to Capeside from New York City. She lived right next door to Dawson with her grandmother. Dawson had been crazed for Jen when she first came to town. It had made Joey insane with jealousy.

That was then, Joey reminded herself. This is now.

"Jen, how would you like it if some guy drooled over you the way you're drooling over him?" Andie chided.

Jen smiled. "That's a joke, right?"

"Okay, so guys drool over you all the time," Andie allowed. "My point is, you are reducing him to a sex object just because he's good-looking and a model."

"I know, I'm terrible," Jen smirked. "Wonder what's under that bathrobe, don't you?" She got up and sauntered across the room to talk to some other classmates.

Andie watched her walk away. "I wonder what it's like to be that self-confident."

"I wouldn't know," Joey admitted.

"Hello, class, so sorry to be late."

Everyone scurried to their seats. The art teacher, Ms. Lewinger, had long, frizzy gray hair, wore a mid-length gray skirt, and Birkenstock sandals—Joey was pretty sure she hadn't shaved her legs since Burn Your Bra Day in 1968.

"Whoa, check her out, serious time warp," Andie whispered. "Which way is Woodstock Nation?"

"Welcome to Advanced Life Drawing," Ms. Lewinger said, smiling broadly. "I hope this class will excite, challenge, and nurture the artist that is inside each and every one of you. Since this is an advanced class, we're going to jump right in with figure drawing."

Joey had experience with figure drawing. In fact, Andie's brother, Jack, had once been her model— her *nude* model.

"You okay?" Andie whispered to Joey. "Your face just turned bright red."

"I'm fine," Joey whispered back. She forced the image of a nude Jack out of her mind and concentrated on what the teacher was saying.

"The human body, in its many variations, is beautiful," Ms. Lewinger continued. "As this class progresses, you'll have the opportunity to draw models of many different sizes and shapes. Our first model is a young man from the community college who has a great deal of experience as an artist's model." She nodded at the handsome guy sitting on a stool. "His name is Aaron Poole."

The tall, rangy guy nodded at the students.

"I think I'm in love," Nicole Graff murmured from her seat on the other side of Andie. Redheaded Nicole was a recent transfer student from a private school. Rumor was she'd gotten thrown out for being too wild.

"Aaron, if you would, please," Ms. Lewinger said.

"Hey, if he would, I would," Nicole quipped.

"Would you please be quiet so we can—" Andie

stopped speaking in mid-sentence. Her jaw hung open.

"What?" Joey asked.

Andie pointed. Joey looked at their model again—and she understood why Andie was blushing.

The model had dropped his robe. And what he was wearing underneath it was . . . nothing. Well, close to nothing, anyway—a very tight, racer-style Speedo bathing suit.

"He's . . . he's . . ." Andie stammered.

"Andie, get a grip," Joey hissed at her. "What do you think figure drawing is?"

"What I want all of you to do is to execute a quick sketch of Aaron," the teacher said. "Take no more than a half hour. Don't edit yourself; let the art flow from inside of you. I'll circulate around the room to offer guidance, but, remember, in my class there is no right and there is no wrong. Please begin."

Joey picked up a piece of charcoal and studied the model. She refused to be embarrassed. Nothing could be as embarrassing as the time Jack had posed for her and his towel had fallen off. Since then, she'd drawn nudes for Professor Harris's class—and drawn them well. Andie, however, still had her jaw hanging open.

"Close your mouth, you're catching flies, McPhee," Nicole said.

Andie clamped her jaw shut, but her eyes still looked as if they were going to pop out of her head.

"Oh, come on," Joey chided her. "You have a brother. It's not like you are totally unfamiliar with male anatomy."

9

"Brothers don't count as male anatomy," Andie said.

"Anyway, he's wearing that horrible little Euro-trash bathing suit thing," Joey added. "He's not even naked."

"He should be," Nicole said, a wicked gleam in her eye. "How's about if we vote on his stripping?"

Joey just shook her head and began to draw, lightly sketching in the line of the model's back, trying to personalize her work as Professor Harris had taught her.

Andie leaned closer to Joey. "Just out of curiosity," she began, "how many naked guys have you seen in your life?"

"Do paintings count?" Joey muted the line she'd just drawn with her art gum eraser.

"Come on, how many?" Andie pressed. "Not counting my brother under any circumstances, because that thought is just too gross for words. Twenty? Four? Any of them named Dawson?"

Joey sketched in one muscular arm. "I grew up with Dawson. Of course I've seen him naked."

"Yeah, but I mean since he . . . grew. Up, I mean."

"Draw, Andie," Joey said.

Andie picked up a pencil and began to sketch. "You think Jen has seen Dawson naked?"

"What Jen has or hasn't seen of Dawson does not concern me in the least."

"You need some work on those lying skills." Andie added a few more lines to her drawing and sighed. "This is starting to look way too groundhog-esque."

Joey tuned Andie out and lost herself in her drawing.

"That's really good," Nicole said, leaning over Joey's drawing.

Joey looked up, startled. She glanced at the clock. She'd been drawing for twenty minutes, but it had seemed like two. She covered her drawing with her hand.

"Oh, sorry," Nicole said. "I was just on my way to the john. You know, your drawing made Mister Model over there look like someone else. Who could it be?" she mused. "Oh, I know. Dawson Leery!" She headed out the door.

Joey looked down at her drawing. Then she looked up at the model. His face morphed into Dawson's. Dawson. Sitting there. Naked. Almost.

Joey blinked twice. The model turned back into Aaron.

He was now staring directly back at Joey.

His gorgeous eyes met hers.

And then he *winked* at her.

Chapter 2

Within a day, the hot, nearly nude model from the Advanced Life Drawing class was the buzz of Capeside High. Every girl who hadn't taken the class was trying to transfer in. The cheerleaders had started a betting pool over how long it would take before the administration kicked out either the model, Ms. Lewinger, or both.

By lunchtime the next day, photocopies of the sketch of Aaron done by Tolliver Heath had multiplied like bacteria; everywhere you looked, there he was. Aaron Poole's awesome form hung on lockers, on bulletin boards, even pinned to the banners advertising the spring dance.

The girls all thought it was great, and, predictably, the guys hated it. Two couples had already broken up when boyfriends had demanded that girlfriends withdraw from Life Drawing. Andie teased Pacey mercilessly about how fine Aaron was, but Joey hadn't said a word to Dawson. Neither had Jen.

As for Dawson, he reminded himself that he wasn't romantically involved with either of them anymore. So why should it bother him if either of them or both of them fell in love or lust with Aaron Poole, male model?

Yeah, right.

"Hey, lucky us, mystery meat again," Pacey said as he and Dawson took trays and got in the hot lunch line. "I'll be opting for the delightful fried fish sandwich and shake instead."

"Unbelievable." Dawson stared at his empty tray.

"I agree. It's been said that human fingers form the foundation of all mystery meat concoctions, but maybe—"

"I meant the tray," Dawson said. "Look at it."

Pacey looked down. Someone had taped a copy of Tolliver's sketch of Aaron to each of the cafeteria trays.

"Not nearly as cute as my father's nudie-girl playing cards," Pacey decided. He covered Aaron's form with his plate of food. "But then politically correct is not my father's middle name. I'm mighty proud of that," he added sarcastically.

"It's sad, really, how easily people get caught up in external appearances," Dawson said after they'd paid for the food and dodged their way through the crowded cafeteria to find seats. They found a table and sat down.

"Oh, yeah, I agree." Pacey arranged the pickle slices from his fishwich as a little bikini top on Aaron's chest in the drawing on his tray.

"Contrary to what people think," Dawson went on, "girls are probably more guilty of that kind of shallowness than guys are." He took a bite of his sandwich. "You'd think we were all still living in caves like Neanderthals, and girls were attracted to whichever Neanderthal has the biggest club."

Pacey laughed, tore off a piece of lettuce, and made Aaron a fig leaf. "Freud would have a field day with that."

"Freud was a cocaine addict," Dawson said. "I am entirely sober and trying to make a point here."

"Which is?"

"Which is, that it's disappointing to discover that girls are guilty of that same small-minded physical objectification of people as sex objects as guys, only more so."

Pacey took a huge slurp of his milkshake. "Look, you might not be Joe Jock, but at least you're blond, tall, and you have that chiseled-chin thing going on. That alone gives you major points in the *True Babe Slam Book of Life*."

Dawson shook his head. "I know I'll regret asking, but what is the *True Babe Slam Book of Life*?"

"Ah, so they haven't let you in on the secret," Pacey said, nodding mysteriously. "There's this secret book where the really gorgeous girls rate guys, then pass it on to their friends. You know, on a scale of one to ten—height, shoulder span, biceps, buns—"

"A mind is a terrible thing to waste, Pacey," Dawson said. "Try to remember that as you travel life's highways and byways."

Pacey flicked the food off Aaron's portrait and

studied it. "Scoff if you will. But Buff Boy down here gets major points in the *True Babe Slam Book of Life*. You of chiseled chin get minor points. And I—alas, poor Pacey, I knew him well—am point-free."

"Come on, Pacey. You've got a great girlfriend—"

"Who just broke a date with me, for like the zillionth time," Pacey said, polishing off his fishwich. "She thinks I put too much pressure on her. I ask you, am I not the last boyfriend on the planet to put pressure on his girlfriend?" He reached into his pocket and took out a cellophane packet containing five or six pills, tore it open, and poured the pills into his hand.

"Better living through chemicals, Pacey?"

"Power-Vites," Pacey explained, noisily swallowing the pills with the last of his milkshake. "A, B-complex, C, D, E, amino acids, creatine, and my particular favorite, two delicious genuine buffalo liver extract tablets. This, my man, is the stuff that dreams are made of. Care to partake?"

Dawson made a face.

"Don't say I didn't offer." Pacey flexed his right bicep. "I feel bigger already. Can you tell?"

"When did you start imbibing that feeble excuse for actual nutrition?"

"Just now," Pacey admitted. "I swiped a few packets from Deputy Doug's lifetime supply before school. He has like a dozen huge containers full of them in the kitchen. He lives on this stuff."

"And since when do you have any desire to do anything that your older brother does?" Dawson asked.

"Since him." Pacey stabbed a finger at Aaron's picture. "Andie, my beloved girlfriend who now needs "space", is hyperventilating over Buff Boy, here."

"Contrary to popular opinion, Pacey, you're smart. Too smart to fall for that body obsession thing."

"Dawson, Dawson, Dawson," Pacey sighed. "I am about to share with you Pacey's First Law of Life. It came to me last night in a dream. Listen carefully. *To the buff go the babes, to the weenies go the woofers.* Thank you and good night."

"To the weenies go the woofers?" Dawson echoed. "Do you hear yourself, Pacey?"

"Loud and clear. Are you going to finish your chips?" Pacey grabbed them. "I need all the calories I can get. Muscle weighs more than fat, you know."

"The only thing fat here is your head. Chew on this, Pacey. Your girlfriend gave you your walking papers, which hurt your ego. So now, just because she spends forty-five minutes a day sketching some brain-dead male model in her art class, you—"

"He's not brain-dead," came a voice from behind Dawson.

Dawson turned around. Not that he didn't know who it was just from the voice. Joey. Looking impossibly cute in her natural, totally Joey way. How was it that a girl in jeans and a baggy sweater carrying a cafeteria tray could make a guy's mouth go dry? This state was helped by the fact that she and Jack weren't even seeing each other anymore . . . Joey was single.

"He's not brain-dead," Joey repeated as she set

her tray on the table. "The model in our art class. He has a name, by the way, which is something the whole school seems to have forgotten. Aaron."

"Yes, but can he spell it?" Dawson joked.

Joey took a bite of her sandwich. "Are we feeling just a little threatened, hmm?"

"That's ludicrous," Dawson sputtered.

Joey just kept chewing.

"Why would I be threatened?" Dawson went on. "I know nothing about this guy, except what he looks like. How could that possibly threaten me?"

"Got me," Joey said, wide-eyed.

"You can be very irritating," Dawson told her.

"Beats being very dishonest," Joey said. "Why can't you just admit it, Dawson? You feel the need to belittle a guy you've never met because he's a handsome model."

"I do not," Dawson snapped.

"Do too," Joey said easily.

"You two are just so *When Harry Met Sally*," Pacey mused. "And by the by, Joey, you're wrong. I know that's an ego blow, o Smug One, but that's the way it is."

"Are you about to enlighten me?" Joey asked.

"Of course," Pacey agreed. "Actually, Dawson is upset because I convinced him he should join me in a fitness program. We made a bet, he lost, so now it's good-bye Body by Spielberg, hello Body by Schwarzenegger."

"That is a figment of your imagination," Dawson said.

"Really?" Pacey asked. "So Joey was right, then,

and you dissed Buff Boy because you felt so threatened?"

Dawson looked from Pacey to Joey. "I give up."

"We start after school today in Deputy Doug's home gym," Pacey told Joey. "Dawson's feeling manly already."

Joey eyed Dawson thoughtfully. "You're really starting a workout program?"

"I don't have a problem with people who choose to spend the valuable and limited time they have enlarging their muscles," Dawson said. "We all make choices about what's really important. And for me, and possibly for any person of real depth and intelligence, the pursuit of physical perfection simply does not compare to the pursuit of art."

"I see," Joey said, nodding. "So if, for example, Girl A, the nonartist, looked something like, say, Uma Thurman, and Girl B, the sensitive artist, looked something like, say, Ricki Lake, and both of these girls really wanted you, Dawson, you're telling me that you'd go for Girl B?"

"That hypothetical example is ridiculous," Dawson replied. "Girl A and Girl B aren't real people—"

"Right, Dawson." Joey crumpled up her sandwich wrapper and stuck it in her paper cup. She got up. "This is a shallow world. Looks are power. Everyone knows it. Unlike you, however, everyone else admits it."

Dawson got up, too. "I know you don't mean that."

How could Joey be this way? She was the one person he'd ever met who cared about what a person was like inside instead of outside.

"Realism is my long suit, Dawson," Joey replied.

"Joey, come on—"

"Tell me why you fell for Jen, then," Joey demanded.

"Because of many things," Dawson began.

Pacey hooted. "You are so busted, Leery!"

"And you two are so *Disturbing Behavior*," Dawson said. "My one-word review is: pathetic. Just because the whole school has had an overnight frontal lobotomy courtesy of Buff Boy the Art Model doesn't mean that you two had to agree to the procedure, too."

Joey smiled. "Like I said, Dawson. You're threatened by Aaron. Big time." She started to walk away.

Dawson watched her walk away, infuriated. "People are not their physical bodies, Joey. I'm disappointed in you."

She kept walking.

"How do you happen to know that Aaron guy has a brain, anyway?" he called.

She turned around and walked backward. "I talked to him," she fibbed.

"So what did he say?" Dawson asked. "Joey? What did he say to you?"

The only answer was Pacey's hilarious laugher. Joey just kept walking.

Chapter 3

"**F**orty-one!" Doug commanded as Dawson and Pacey struggled through the stomach crunches. "Repeat! Forty-one!"

Dawson didn't have enough breath left to respond. In fact, if he tried to speak, he knew it would only come out as a groan, so he kept his mouth shut. His knees had never looked so far away.

"I can't hear you, worms!" Doug yelled.

"This is not a scene from *An Officer and a Gentleman*, Dougie dearest," Pacey managed between grunts.

"You're fat, you're lazy, and you're pasty-faced!" Doug boomed.

"I hate fat, lazy, and pasty-faced," Andie said, grinning mischievously from her spot at the bottom of the basement stairs. "Come on, Pacey, you can do it!"

"Real men count their crunches!" Doug hollered. "Now, let me hear it—forty-two!"

"Forty-two," Pacey managed.

Dawson didn't get beyond opening his mouth and gasping like a newly caught fish. He was just grateful that he wasn't suffering this humiliation in front of Joey or Jen, the way Pacey was suffering it in front of Andie.

"Forty-three!" Doug counted off. "Let's hear it!"

"No more," Dawson gasped. He fell heavily onto his back, his head banging against the thin blue exercise mat.

"Forty-three!" Pacey managed.

"My heeee-ro!" Andie trilled comically.

"Forty-four!" Pacey grunted.

Dawson turned his head on the mat and watched the sweat pour off Pacey's beet red face. And for what? To impress a girl who wanted "space"?

"Forty-five, worm!" Doug yelled.

"Pacey, Pacey, he's our man, if he can't do it, no one can!" Andie cheered.

"Check it out, I'm still going, Dawson. Power set coming up! Forty-six, forty-seven, forty-eight—"

"Go, Pacey!" Doug shouted. "Show your slug of a friend what you've got, gimme fifty!"

"Give him fifty!" Andie echoed. She was literally jumping up and down.

Pacey groaned so loud now that he sounded as if he was giving birth. His body shook as his elbows headed for his knees.

"Fifty, come on!" Doug yelled.

Almost, almost . . .

Pacey fell back against the mat, defeated.

"I should have known," Doug said, disgusted. "When the going got tough, you wimped out. The women cops can do fifty crunches in their sleep."

"Let's not carry the macho-man thing too far," Pacey said, breathing huge gulps of air. "All you gay guys really overcompensate."

"I didn't know you were gay, Doug," Andie said, sitting down again.

"I'm not. It's my little brother's concept of a joke."

Pacey got up on one elbow. "And it would be mighty funny if it weren't so tragically true." He wiped his sweaty forehead with the bottom of his T-shirt and looked over at the exhausted Dawson. "Am I studly or what?"

Dawson sat up. "I can't believe I let you talk me into this. I was supposed to be doing a video chronicle of your transformation—"

"Hey, I knew you wouldn't be able to resist once I got you over here," Pacey said, grinning. "You need a little building up there, Dawson."

Dawson scrambled up from the mat. "Thanks, but I'll pass."

"Too bad," Andie said. "Joey would appreciate the results."

"Try to retain this information, Andie," Dawson said. "Joey and I are friends. Best friends. Best friends don't judge each other on the basis of how many crunches they can do." He got his jacket and picked up his video camera. "Got it?"

"I'm taking mental notes," Andie assured him dryly.

"Lucky for you two I walked in while you were

using my gym equipment," Doug said. He picked up the book Pacey had taken out of the library, *Bodybuilding for Beginners, Weaklings, and Losers*, and brandished it at his brother. "You didn't really expect to learn bodybuilding from this thing, did you?"

"The thought had crossed my mind," Pacey replied.

Doug awkwardly put his arm around his little brother. "Why go to a half-baked book when I can help you? I think this is great, Pacey. I'll run your fitness program. We'll finally have something in common."

Pacey looked sideways at his brother. "The thing that's really frightening me is, you mean it."

"Of course I do, if you'll stick with it."

Great. Deputy Doug wanted to be his personal trainer. And since he intended to use Doug's equipment, he couldn't very well say no. "Hey, commitment is my middle name," Pacey said.

"It's never too late for a fresh start," Doug said, clapping Pacey so hard on the back he almost fell over. "I'm almost proud of you."

"I'm almost touched," Pacey said.

"Now, assume the position and give me twenty, worm!" Doug screamed like a Marine drill sergeant in Pacey's face.

Dawson and Pacey looked at him, askance.

"Just kidding." Doug smiled. "I'm gonna go upstairs and change into some shorts before we move on to the pecs bench. Chest press, incline chest press, decline chest press, chest flies, all right!" He pounded Pacey on the back again and bounded up the stairs.

"I might be coming down with something," Pacey said, feeling his forehead.

Andie ran over to him and gave him a quick hug. "I'm so proud of you. Gotta run, but it was great watching you."

"Oh, right," Pacey said, wondering what an incline chest press was, and how much it hurt.

"So, I'll call you later, or you call me, or whatever," Andie said. "Bye!" She ran upstairs.

Pacey fell onto the mat. "I might not live through this." He looked up. Dawson had the video camera aimed at him. "What, now you're getting footage?"

"So what was it like, being humiliated by your big brother and trying to live up to some mythical concept of masculinity in front of your girlfriend who wants space?" Dawson asked, filming away. "Is this supposed to make her decide that you're the only guy for her? Do you build confidence with muscle?"

"Feel free to hide behind your little lens, per usual, Dawson," Pacey said. "Just remember, to the buff go the babes, to the weenies go—"

"That is so not true," Dawson interrupted, putting the camera down.

"The truth hurts, my man." Pacey wiped his forehead again. "Would you go out with Emily LaPaz?"

"You mean Emily from bio lab?"

Pacey nodded. "The one and only. Nice girl. Smart. A butt the size of New Jersey. Would you go out with her?"

"I don't really know her well enough to—"

"All right, on your feet!" Doug cried out as he bounded down the stairs. In his right hand, he held two plastic bottles of some kind of reddish liquid. He tossed one bottle to Pacey and one to Dawson.

Dawson stared at it. "What is this?"

"CarboGas," Doug replied. "Six hundred and twenty-five calories per bottle. I drink two of 'em a day. Replaces those essential lost electrolytes, et cetera, et cetera." He reached into his shorts pocket and took out two cellophane packets, identical to the one that Pacey had brought to school that morning.

"Take this with the CarboGas," Doug advised them, chucking Dawson and his brother each one of the packets. "The combo is dynamite. It'll make you big, strong, fast."

"Which leads me to ask, what if you don't want to be big?" Dawson asked. "What if you're okay with yourself just as you are?"

"You are?" Doug asked, astonished.

"I fail to see what is essentially superior about muscle mass," Dawson explained.

"Well, Dawson, it's been true throughout history that physically superior specimens thrive, and physically inferior specimens die out." Doug picked up two ten-pound weight plates and placed them on the ends of a forty-five-pound Olympic bar balanced above the pecs bench.

"Biology is hardly destiny," Dawson said.

"Agreed." Doug made sure the weights were balanced. "That is why real men work to be physically superior."

"To the buff go the babes—" Pacey began.

"You know, there is more of your brother in you than you would like to believe," Dawson told Pacey.

Pacey popped the handful of pills into his mouth, then swallowed them by draining the entire bottle of CarboGas. Then he belched. Loudly.

"Lovely," Dawson told him. "Too bad Andie missed it."

Pacey crushed the empty plastic bottle in his hand. "I'm getting an Incredible Hulk sort of feeling already."

"That's the spirit, bro," Doug told him. "So, you ready to go from Pillsbury Doughboy to Real Man?"

Pacey jumped up and saluted his brother.

Dawson took in the gung-ho look on Pacey's face and slapped his unopened cellophane packet into Pacey's hand. "For later."

"You're missing out, Dawson," Doug told him.

"I'll risk it. Catch you later, Pacey."

Dawson climbed the stairs and let himself out to the sound of Doug barking commands at Pacey.

No doubt about it. Pacey was losing his mind.

It was a terrifying nightmare.

Misery. The movie. Where James Caan was an author tied to a bed by Kathy Bates, who plays an insane fan. Only in Dawson's dream, it wasn't Kathy Bates standing over Dawson, it was Deputy Doug, standing on a balcony, and he was launching heavy cinderblocks down on Dawson's exposed stomach.

"To the buff go the babes, weenie-boy!" Doug kept yelling as he maniacally hurled cinderblock after cinderblock at Dawson. "Gotta build up them abs!"

"No! No more!" Dawson screamed as Doug was about to launch three cinderblocks at once. But Doug just laughed, and the cinderblocks careened downward, heading right for him, and—

Aaaargh!

"Dawson! Honey, are you okay?"

Dawson opened his eyes. A nightmare. He had been having the most terrible nightmare.

"Dawson?" his mom called through his door.

"Yeah, I'm up," he called back. He tried to sit up. He felt as if he'd been punched in the stomach. And the pecs. And the quads of his legs. And the delts of his shoulders.

Everything hurt.

"Deputy Doug," he groaned, lying back down again.

"I'm late for the station. There's breakfast on the table," Gale Leery called. "You're running late yourself, so I suggest you get a move on. See you, sweetie."

Slowly, as pain radiated through his body, Dawson sat up. In the olden days, before his father had moved out—no, before his mother had cheated on his father, which had led to his father's moving out—it wouldn't have made much difference if he was running late. His dad would have happily driven him to school.

Dawson felt a fresh pain, just thinking about his absent dad. It hurt a lot more than too much working out.

But he couldn't think about that now. Somehow he had to force his body into a hot shower and get to school.

27

After he'd managed the herculean task of showering and dressing—putting ancient loafers on his feet instead of sneakers just so he wouldn't have to bend over to tie his shoes—he hobbled downstairs. Each step sent a bolt of agony to his thighs. He had no interest in breakfast, but he was pretty sure his mom kept some aspirin in the kitchen cabinet.

To his surprise, Jen was sitting at his kitchen table, reading the newspaper. "Famine, floods, and dirty politics," Jen said. "I ask you, Dawson, how do people voluntarily read the newspaper first thing in the morning?"

"Good morning to you, too," Dawson said. He opened the cupboard and rummaged.

"I saw your mom outside," Jen explained. "She said you were running late, so I asked Grams if she'd give us both a ride to school. She said fine. The trade-off is we'll have to listen to inspirational tapes on the way."

"Uh-huh." All Dawson could think about was finding aspirin. Ah, there it was. Three ought to do the trick. He filled a mug with water and took them.

"So, it occurs to me that you aren't quite yourself this morning," Jen observed.

"I'm fine." His backpack was on the other counter. Which meant walking to the other counter. The other counter was across the universe. He'd rest first. He made it to the table and sat down.

"Are you limping?"

"I may have stubbed my toe," Dawson answered lamely.

"Really. Wow, must have been some stub, huh?"

"Must have been," Dawson managed. His mom

had left a glass of orange juice for him on the table. He picked it up and winced before the glass got to his lips.

"So, did you stub your arm, too?" Jen asked.

"I don't want to be rude, Jen, but I'm not up to conversation."

"That's okay," she assured him. "You know, I heard the funniest thing last night. Andie called me about some homework, and she said you and Pacey had started working out together in Pacey's basement."

"She said that?"

"She did." Jen got up and sauntered around the kitchen as she spoke. "I pointed out that you were far too cerebral, and Pacey was far too lazy, so it had to be a figment of her overactive imagination. Right, Dawson?"

She was standing directly behind his chair now.

"Oh well, you know Andie," Dawson managed.

"So, I was thinking," Jen went on softly from behind him, "that if you had started working out with Pacey, you'd probably be really sore this morning." Her hands landed lightly on his shoulders. "Wouldn't you?"

Dawson froze. It wasn't that he didn't enjoy Jen's touch, because he did. There was a time, in fact, when he would have done almost anything for it. But then she'd broken up with him. And then there was Joey. And now there was . . .

Well, who knew what there was now? Or what he wanted? Or what *she* wanted?

Slowly, Jen's fingers began to knead the sore muscles of his shoulders. "I knew this incredible woman back in New York," Jen said, her voice low. "She was from Sweden. She gave the most amazing massages. My mother and her New York society buds paid a fortune to have this woman work on them. I went to her once, and I still remember everything she did."

A soft groan escaped from between Dawson's lips. His head began to loll. He was so sore. It felt so *good.* He could smell Jen's perfume, the same one he remembered from that time when he'd held her in his arms, and—

"Do I look like a taxi service with my meter running?"

Jen's grandmother was standing inside the open kitchen door. Dawson jumped up as if she'd caught them passionately making out. His whole body vibrated with pain.

"Sorry, Grams," Jen said, reaching for her backpack. "Dawson had a problem, and I was trying to help."

"I'd say the both of you have a problem, and the both of you need to get to school where you can be properly supervised," Grams replied sharply.

"Right, school," Dawson said, reaching for his own backpack, his muscles screaming, his face red with embarrassment. "It's really nice of you to drive us."

Dawson took small, sliding steps toward the door.

"Well, get a move on, young man, I haven't got all day," Jen's grandmother snapped.

"Right, sorry." Dawson willed his legs to move faster. He made it out the door and headed for her car, Jen beside him. Grams walked briskly ahead of them, then turned back. "The back door is broken on the passenger side, young man," she said. "So you'll have to climb into the backseat."

"I'll do it," Jen said quickly. "You sit in front, Dawson."

Grams got into the car, a look of stern disapproval on her face. "In my day a boy would never sit in the front and let a girl sit in the back. And a well-brought-up boy opened the car door for a girl, too." She started the car.

"Dawson isn't feeling too well this morning, Grams," Jen explained.

"Well, then, you had better keep your distance so that you don't catch whatever he's got, hadn't you?" Grams replied. She pushed a cassette in, and a preacher harangued them about the wages of sin all the way to Capeside High.

Chapter 4

"**O**ne double-banana, double-chocolate milk-shake to go," Joey said, setting a huge Styrofoam cup down in front of Pacey. "A zillion calories, certified by my sister Bessie, chef extraordinaire of the infamous Ice House, restaurant to the stars."

"That certainly applies to you, Pacey," Dawson teased from his seat at the counter.

"Hey, today a pasty-faced clown, tomorrow a muscle-bound babe magnet," Pacey said. "Hollywood will follow shortly thereafter. When Barbara Walters interviews me on Oscar night, I will probably have forgotten both of your names. Cheers." He took a large guzzle of his shake.

Dawson watched him skeptically. He was amazed that Pacey had stuck to his fitness program for five days straight. To Dawson's knowledge, that was the longest Pacey had ever stuck to anything.

32

"Are you ordering, Dawson?" Joey asked, sticking her pencil behind her ear. "Or are you just sitting there taking up space?"

"He's coming with me to work out, right?" Pacey asked, snapping a lid on what was left of his milkshake so he could take it with him.

"Thanks, but I'll pass," Dawson said.

"You lasted, what, Dawson, two days?" Joey asked.

"It wasn't a matter of lasting," Dawson corrected her. "Working out is a fundamentally shallow pursuit, essentially meaningless."

"He lasted one day," Pacey said, ignoring Dawson. "But it was a gem. It really added to the experience to hear those patented Dawson animal grunts from the creature next to me on the mat."

"Tape it for me next time," Joey said. "I need more fun in my life." She hurried off to wait on a customer.

"Her sense of humor borders on the caustic," Dawson observed. "She's deeply compensating."

Pacey picked up his milkshake. "Analyze away, my man. Meanwhile, I, Pacey Witter, will be doing instead of thinking, and changing my life."

"That's an illusion, Pacey. Real change is, by definition, internal, not external."

"Let me know when you join us here on Planet Capeside," Pacey said, saluting Dawson with his milkshake. "And now, I've gotta run. My latissimus dorsi muscles are clamoring for personal attention."

"Just make sure all this new muscle doesn't edge out whatever brains you have left, okay?" Dawson called.

Pacey growled and hit a muscle pose, then he headed out the door, just as Bessie came out of the kitchen and put a large Greek salad in front of Dawson. Dawson had ordered it before Joey arrived to start her shift. His mom was working late at the station, where she was a local news anchor, so she'd called and told him to nuke leftovers or eat dinner at the Ice House. Dawson hadn't been able to face leftovers in his silent, lonely home. It was just too sad.

Dawson took a bite of a hot pepper. During the last week, it seemed he'd eaten more meals at the counter of the Ice House than at the table of his own house. Fortunately, the place was nearly empty—just one other lone diner at the other end of the counter and a couple of off-season tourists on the floor of the restaurant. At least the rest of Capeside didn't have to see that he was eating dinner solo, again.

Dawson sighed and opened his sociology book. They were studying deviance. Did eating meal after meal by yourself at the local diner, when your mother and father were *not* dead, constitute some kind of deviance?

"Oh, so you did order," Joey said, putting the tourists' order ticket up on the rack. "Dining solo again, are we?"

"You could join me," Dawson suggested.

Joey shook her head no. "Sitting while on duty is a first-class felony. Automatic death penalty, according to my sister the boss."

"And your sister the boss suggests that you move your backpack off the prep counter," Bessie said, her arms full of salt and pepper shakers. "You know your books don't belong there."

"If my punishment is waitressing here for the rest

of my life, I might prefer the death penalty." Joey shoved her backpack under the counter, but not before Dawson noticed her sketchbook from art class that was under it.

"How's Advanced Life Drawing?" Dawson asked casually.

"Aaron and I are running away to a South Seas island where the men don't wear clothes," Joey cracked. "Why?"

"I asked you a perfectly civil question, Joey—"

"And I made a joke. A pox on my house."

"Forget it. Forget I cared enough to ask." Dawson stabbed a tomato with his fork.

Joey leaned against the counter, watching him. "I'm sorry," she finally said. "I have irritable human syndrome tonight. The truth is, I'm in an art slump. I want to be able to draw. I really do. And I'm trying. I can see exactly what I want to do in my mind. But what comes out on paper does not remotely resemble the image in my mind. In other words, I suck."

Dawson nodded seriously, but inside he felt sunshine breaking out. So, her concern was over her art and not over Aaron. This was good news. Excellent news, even.

"You have talent, Joey," Dawson insisted. "Everyone says so."

"Yeah, everyone but me." She leaned over to change the radio station from classic rock to the National Public Radio affiliate. The sound of a cello filled the air, a piece by Pablo Casals.

"Order up!" Bessie called. Joey picked up the hot plates and took them to the tourists.

Dawson closed his eyes and listened to the music, his head filled with a girl named Katrina Turner. Dawson had been walking by the band room the week before, when he'd heard someone playing that same piece. Curious, he'd opened the door. And there sat this girl—slender, graceful, her long auburn hair swaying in rhythm to the incredible music she was creating with her cello. She'd been lost in her music and hadn't even noticed him. But he'd asked about her. She was a senior, a transfer student.

Katrina Turner. He thought about her a lot.

Dawson looked up to find Joey staring at him. "Does the music make visions of sugarplums dance in your head, Dawson? Or could it be visions of a certain auburn-haired senior who does not know that Dawson Leery exists?"

He'd made the mistake of confiding in Joey about Katrina. She'd been teasing him about it ever since.

"Talent is extremely appealing," Dawson said. "Isn't that why you want to be a good artist?"

"No. I want to be a good artist for myself, not to appeal to anyone else."

"I don't think you're being entirely honest with yourself, Joey. You want to be a good artist for the same reason that Pacey wants muscles."

Joey slammed her palm on the counter. "You know I hate it when you do this, don't you?"

"Do what?"

"Your endless, supercilious analysis of my life and motivations. And you're doing it now to deflect the conversation away from Katrina Turner. Because, Dawson, you do not want to admit why you are attracted to her, to wit: her talent is entirely secondary to her amazingly great looks."

Dawson put down his fork. "You underestimate me. Talent is sexy. All you have to do is look at a filmmaker like Woody Allen. He's had endless desirable women."

Joey tapped her finger on Dawson's sociology book.

"Just a little tip, Dawson. About deviant behavior. There ought to be an entire section in your book under the chapter heading 'Woody Allen.' And I wouldn't be holding Woody Allen up as a paragon of male sex appeal if I were you."

"Okay, forget Woody Allen. All I'm saying is that when I first heard Katrina play, I couldn't see her. But the music was so beautiful that I was swept away."

"*Swept Away*, Lina Wertmüller, great movie," Joey said. "We saw it on movie night, if I recall correctly. Let's see, on a desert island, the rich woman falls for the poor guy because he's so hot-looking, but when they're back in civilization, she ignores him. Hmm."

Dawson stared at Joey, who leaned against the counter, her arms folded. She was wearing this blue sweater that he really liked on her. How could she be so irritating and so appealing at the same time? And why was he thinking about how appealing Joey was when she was irritating him about another girl he found really appealing?

Dawson took a deep breath. He was not going to let Joey get to him. "What I'm trying to say, Joey," he said slowly, "is that if a person is truly evolved, then the physical is essentially secondary to the attraction of—yeccch!"

An incredibly foul odor permeated the Ice House, something like a mixture of raw sewage and fermented fish guts.

"What is that?" Joey asked, whirling around, trying hard not to gag. "Bessie!" she yelled into the kitchen.

"Waitress, waitress, bring our check!" the tourists yelled frantically.

Joey ran to the table with the check as the guy at the other end of the counter bolted for the door and took off without paying, holding a handkerchief to his nose. Bessie and Jack McPhee, Andie's older brother who worked part-time at the Ice House, ran out of the kitchen. Both of them had their hands over their noses and mouths.

"What is it?" Dawson demanded.

"Sewage backup!" Bessie gasped. "Look!"

She pointed at the sink behind the counter. It was filled with a noxious tar-colored pool of raw sewage that was rising quickly.

The tourists threw some money on their table and ran out of the restaurant.

"God, it reeks," Joey said.

"I am so screwed," Bessie groaned from behind her hand. "I was afraid that this would happen someday."

"Can't you fix it?" Dawson asked.

"Oh, sure," Bessie answered. "If I had a spare five thou in the bank collecting dust, which I don't. The health department is going to shut the Ice House down in the morning, and there's not a damn thing we can do about it."

Chapter 5

Joey reached into the back pocket of her jeans and unfolded the sign she'd hand-lettered with a Magic Marker. She flattened it against the front door of the Ice House.

"Tape," she called to Dawson, who was standing on the sidewalk, talking with Jen. Pacey was busy making muscles, admiring the new dimensions of his biceps.

Dawson hurried over with the tape and quickly put up the sign: ICE HOUSE CLOSED TEMPORARILY. THANK YOU FOR YOUR UNDERSTANDING.

Joey gazed at it, her hands buried in her pockets.

"Maybe I should have added a postscript, such as: 'As the Ice House will not reopen in the near future due to lack of funds, anyone who knows of a visible means of support for the owner and her kid sister, please row over to the wrong side of the creek and scream loudly in the direction of the house in the worst state of disrepair. Thank you.' "

"Come on, Joey," Dawson said. "We'll figure out a way to get the Ice House open soon. It's not that bad."

"It is that bad," Joey said. "I know it's a difficult concept for you and Miss New York Condo to grasp—"

"Thanks a lot," Jen interrupted.

"And Pacey hasn't grasped anything since puberty," Joey continued, "but here's the deal. Bessie and I are broke. As in busted. As in where's the nearest food stamp line. So unless you happen to have studied plumbing between films, don't offer me meaningless platitudes."

Dawson didn't reply. He knew she was right. The first estimate Bessie had gotten to redo the pipes for the Ice House was more than eight thousand dollars.

"Maybe we could do something to raise the money," Jen suggested.

"Great idea," Joey said sarcastically. "We could be like Judy Garland and Mickey Rooney and put on a show. Gosh, but those old movies are keen. Love that realism."

"Look, sarcasm isn't going to get us anywhere," Jen said. "Maybe if we—"

"I hesitate to point this out to you, Jen, but there is no 'us' here," Joey said. It was a cold, gray day, as befitted her mood, and she stuck her hands under the armpits of her sweatshirt to warm them up. "You have parents who still send a small fortune to keep you in designer clothes. Pacey may be a slug, but he's a slug whose father is the chief of police. Last time I checked, that was a regular job—"

"Albeit a frightening one," Pacey put in.

"And Dawson's mom earns more in a month as a TV anchor then Bessie earns in a year."

"Okay, you're right," Jen acknowledged. She couldn't help it; even though Joey was often rude to her, sometimes even downright nasty, she still liked her. Admired her, really. That is, when she wasn't busy feeling jealous about her relationship with Dawson. Whatever *that* was these days.

"I have to figure out a way to get us some major money," Joey said, "and get it fast."

That afternoon after school, Dawson, Jen, Pacey, Andie, and Joey had met up with Bessie and Jack at the Ice House. Armed with rubber gloves and thick paper masks, they'd worked for three hours to clean up the backed-up sewage. It coated the entire kitchen with a thick, yucky, disgusting slime. Bessie had used what little savings she had to pay for a septic-tank truck to cart away the slime they collected.

Andie had to get home right after they finished, Bessie had to relieve a friend who was watching the baby, and Jack had disappeared, too. The four of them had gone back to Dawson's, showered and changed into clean clothes they'd brought with them, then come back to the Ice House to put up the sign.

Joey leaned against the tree in front of the restaurant, not noticing that the first buds of spring were greening up the tree's branches. Instead, the image of her sister, dashing from the restaurant with tears streaming down her face, filled Joey's mind. Bessie was the strongest person Joey knew. Bessie never cried. Bessie never panicked.

It was bad enough that their mom was dead and their dad was in jail and that Bessie was, at the moment, raising Alexander all by herself. To see her sister reduced to tears the way she had been a couple of hours ago—it tore at Joey's heart. And scared her, in some deep place that she tried not to visit.

Pacey brought over the ice cooler full of sodas and bottles of juice he'd lugged from Dawson's house. He took out a raspberry CarboGas for himself and tossed Joey a bottle of flavored ice tea.

"You're still drinking that red swill?" Dawson asked him, eyeing the CarboGas.

"This swill, as you refer to it, allowed me, the great buff Pacey, to do three times the work of you, the weenie Dawson." Pacey cracked open the CarboGas. "Anyway, I've got to get my system juiced for my evening workout."

Andie touched Pacey's left bicep. "Am I supposed to feel a difference?"

"You wound me," Pacey replied.

Andie shrugged and reached into the cooler for a Coke.

"I can spare my princely salary from ScreenPlay," Pacey offered, "if that'll help."

"Thanks anyway," Joey replied.

"Okay, how about a benefit concert?" Dawson suggested brightly. "Or a telethon? Maybe my mom can get the television station to—"

"Dawson, the Ice House is not Greenpeace or starving children in Somalia or an Armenian earth-

quake fund," Joey said. "No one has a benefit concert for a two-bit little restaurant with backed-up
sewer lines. It lacks a certain *cachet.*"

Dawson sighed. She was right.

"I've got a trust fund," Jen said quietly.

Everyone's eyes swung to her.

"I don't get access to it until I'm eighteen," Jen
continued sadly. "But I'd lend it to you if I had it."

The phrase "Talk is cheap" sprang into Joey's
mind, but she forced herself not to say it. Because
maybe Jen was actually telling the truth.

"There has to be a way out of this," Dawson insisted. "A bank loan, maybe. Don't banks make
loans to businesses?"

"Not businesses that are already in debt," Joey
replied. "Bessie is going to have to find a job, and
so am I. And we'll just try to earn enough money
to get the Ice House open again."

"But what if you don't earn enough?" Jen asked.

Joey slid down the tree and looked up at her
homemade sign on the front of the restaurant: TEM-
PORARILY CLOSED. "I have no idea," she admitted.
"No idea at all."

Joey awoke with a start. Her heart was pounding.
It was a Sunday morning. The room was way too
bright. Meaning the sun was way too high. Meaning
she'd somehow slept right through her alarm and
missed the Sunday breakfast rush at—

And then she remembered. There was no Sunday
breakfast rush at the Ice House. Because there was
no Ice House.

Joey got out of bed, pulled on a clean T-shirt and

some jeans, and padded into the small living room. Bessie was huddled over a table in the corner, the Help Wanted ads from the Sunday newspaper spread out on the floor to one side of her, a bunch of bank statements and a check ledger on the table in front of her. The baby was in his playpen, teething and drooling on a cloth book.

"See anything good?" Joey asked as she poured herself some coffee.

"Not unless I can fool a hospital in Boston into believing I'm a brain surgeon," Bessie replied without looking up. The baby began to fuss. "Can you get Alex a bottle?"

Joey took a bottle from the fridge and stuck it in the microwave to heat. "I don't suppose we could get a bank loan."

"Dream on."

Joey scooped her nephew out of his playpen and sat on the couch to give him his bottle. He gurgled happily. "Gee, easy to make you happy, big guy."

Bessie looked over at her son. Her eyes were bloodshot, with dark circles under them like two bruised moons. Her hair was a mess. She looked old and worn-out, even though she was only in her early twenties. It made Joey shudder.

"He's such a good baby," Bessie said fondly. "He's so cute." An idea hit her. "Hey, maybe Alex could model, you know, do print ads or baby food commercials?"

"I'm going to assume that you aren't serious." Joey shifted the baby to a better angle.

"Yeah, I'd never exploit my kid that way," Bessie

agreed. "Chalk it up to temporary insanity." She buried her head in the want ads again.

The baby finished. Joey put him over her shoulder to burp him. Usually she hated taking care of Alex. It wasn't that she didn't love her nephew, it was that she resented feeling she'd somehow become a co-parent. But now Bessie was in so much trouble that resenting Alex was the last thing on Joey's mind.

Alex burped. "Good boy," Joey said. She turned to her sister. "So, what time did you wake up?"

"Actually, I didn't go to sleep. Want to hear the damage?" Bessie pointed to the bank statements.

"I can take it if you can," Joey replied, setting Alex back in the playpen.

"There's good news and bad news," Bessie said. "The good news is that we're not going to be homeless for at least the next forty-five days, and the bad news is that you can plan on eating a lot of macaroni and cheese during that time."

"And after that?" Joey asked.

"After that is what kept me up all night," Bessie admitted.

Joey held her hand out. "Toss me the want ads."

"I've gone through them already. There are some restaurants looking for kitchen help. I've got them circled. I'll start calling tomorrow morning."

"I didn't mean for you, I meant for me," Joey said.

"Part-time only, Capeside only, nothing that interferes with your schoolwork," Bessie declared. "Deal?"

"You are in no position to play *Lets Make a*

Deal, Bessie. You and I both know that if we don't make the repairs on the Ice House, we lose it."

"I mean it, Joey—"

"Just give me the newspaper."

Bessie held the want ads behind her back, her eyes blazing. "I swear to you, Joey, I will beat you up myself before I let you take some stupid job that interferes with school. I promised Mom you'd go to college, and you know it. If you think I'm going back on a deathbed promise to her, you have another think coming. Now, do we have a deal?"

Their eyes locked.

"Deal." Joey finally relented.

Bessie handed her the paper and went to change Alexander's diaper. Joey spread the paper out and scanned the part-time listings.

BABYSITTER. During school hours for working mother.

BABYSITTER. During school hours for working mother.

HOUSECLEANER. Must work during the day.

"It's all daytime," Joey complained, sipping her coffee. "Here's one. Night clerk at the Parkway Motel."

"No way, Joey, they rent rooms by the hour for quickies," Bessie said.

Just then the phone rang.

"I'll get it." Joey padded over to the phone and answered it. "Hello?"

"Joey, it's Jen."

"Don't tell me. You turned eighteen, and your trust fund is now available."

"I wish. Listen, did you see the paper today? The Help Wanted section?"

"I was inhaling it when you called, actually. I can drop out of school to baby-sit or watch over the illicit mating habits of the unhappily married at a no-tell motel."

"I saw a job listed that's perfect for you," Jen said.

"Are we talking about the same newspaper?"

"Get it, okay?"

"Hold on a sec." Joey put the phone down and got the newspaper, then she came back and cradled it between her ear and her shoulder. "Okay, which ad has my name on it?"

"Page H–14, about halfway down, third column from the right," Jen said.

Joey scanned the page. "Let's see . . . 'Mechanic. Must have own tools to work on heavy equipment. Menial laborer in sausage-packing plant, third shift . . .'"

"Lower, Joey," Jen instructed.

And there it was:

MODELS WANTED. European catalog distributor seeks fresh faces for upcoming editions. Must be photogenic, size 6–8, at least 5'7". No nudity. Excellent pay. Call 555–3451 for information and Boston area go-see.

"Joey?" Jen called into the phone. "Are you there? Did you see the modeling ad?"

Dawson's image flashed into Joey's mind. Dawson, with his ridiculous ideas about how a person isn't who they are on the outside but who they are on the inside. What could be more blatantly exploitive of your outside than having someone pay you for sexy photos of yourself?

Besides, I am so not cute enough, Joey thought. Which is exactly what she told Jen.

"You're wrong, Joey," Jen replied. "I had some friends who modeled part-time in New York. You're taller than they are, and you have a better body."

"Get out of here!" Joey exclaimed, momentarily at a loss for words.

"I mean it," Jen insisted. "Remember when I told you to enter the Miss Windjammer pageant? I was right about that, wasn't I?"

"No. I lost."

"You came in second," Jen reminded her. "Meaning you almost won. Face it, Joey, how you think you look and reality are light-years apart. You can definitely—"

"Jen, where are you?" Joey heard Jen's grandmother calling through the phone. "We need to leave!"

"Joey, I gotta run. So, will you think about it?"

"I don't know."

"I'm telling you, catalog work pays great, if it's legit," Jen insisted.

"What's great?"

"Great is it could pay to fix the pipes in the Ice House, or damn close to it. And if it's not legit, then you walk away."

"Jen!" Grams called again.

"Gotta run, Joey. Think about it."

"I already have. Forget it."

"Whatever," Jen said. "Just trying to help out."

Joey said good-bye and hung up. Modeling? Joey Potter? She couldn't even dance with a cute guy without feeling self-conscious. Maybe Jen had only told her about the modeling gig so she'd try for it and get shut down.

Nah. Joey knew that wasn't true. As much as she wanted to attribute such ugly motivations to Jen, she couldn't. Jen was serious.

"Seriously deluded," Joey mumbled, heading back to the living room. Bessie was inputting something into the calculator.

"So, we have enough extra for that big Paris vacation?" Joey joked, plopping down on the threadbare couch.

"Who was on the phone?"

"Dawson," Joey lied. "He was calling to see if we wanted to make a family excursion to Goodwill Industries, then swing by the local homeless shelter."

"Not funny," Bessie snapped. "I'm doing my best here, okay? I didn't ask for this, you know."

Guilt stabbed through Joey. Bessie was right. None of this was Bessie's fault. It just . . . it just was.

Jocy cycd thc modeling ad again. What if Jen was right?

Do I have the nerve to actually try? Joey asked herself. I would feel like the biggest dweeb, geek, idiot girl in the world. And whoever it is that auditions models would laugh and throw me out on my butt.

My tall, skinny butt. ". . . size 6-8, at least 5'7"," Joey read again.

"Find anything?" Bessie asked.

"Sausage-packing plant, third shift," Joey replied.

Or catalog model, Joey added in her mind. But somehow she could picture herself getting hired to stuff sausage before she could see herself getting hired to model.

Chapter 6

The bell rang, signaling the end of Advanced Life
Drawing class, but Joey stayed at her desk, completely absorbed in her almost-completed drawing
of Aaron Poole.

Some shading on the hollow of his thigh. Soften
that line. Shade some more. Get the perfect play of
light, the subtle tones of his muscles . . .

She was oblivious to the noise outside the art
room; she just drew on.

Advanced Life Drawing had become Joey's all-
too-brief respite from her worries. She lost herself
in art; everything else faded away. There was no
Dawson, no money problems, no dad in jail, no
worries about how the hell she was ever going to
get out and stay out of Capeside.

She was also starting to believe that she just might
have some talent. Not a lot, but some. After all, Ms.

Lewinger wasn't the first person who was supposed to know something about art who had encouraged her. But then Ms. Lewinger probably had taken one too many acid trips in the sixties, so maybe she didn't count.

Joey softened the shading with the edge of her art gum eraser. She cocked her head sideways, studying the curved line of his—

"Joey?"

She looked up, startled.

Ms. Lewinger stood behind her, looking down at her pad.

Unconsciously, Joey put her hands atop her drawing, trying to prevent her teacher from looking at it.

"Class is over," the teacher said softly.

"How long have you been watching me?" Joey asked self-consciously.

"Not long." Ms. Lewinger wore the same long wool skirt she had worn the first day of class and had added a fuzzy, no-color vest and a necklace of tiny silver peace symbols. Joey couldn't help but note that her art teacher had very hairy arms.

"Artists rarely want their works-in-progress seen," Ms. Lewinger said. "I understand."

Joey bit her lower lip. This was her third attempt to capture Aaron. Ms. Lewinger hadn't seen this one yet. Joey reluctantly moved her hands.

The teacher studied her drawing and then audibly blew a gentle stream of air through her pursed lips.

"I know, it needs work," Joey told her. She felt blood rush to her face and her stomach knotted up.

"Yes, of course it does," Ms. Lewinger agreed.

"But it's also quite wonderful. Your technique is immature, of course, but you're improving steadily."

Joey felt a rush of happiness. "Thanks."

"You're welcome. You're a true artist, Joey. Has anyone ever told you that?"

"Kind of," Joey admitted. "It's hard to believe, though." A new thought hit her. "Wait, you're not just doing one of those 'everything is beautiful' things they did in the sixties, are you? You know, like where you weren't supposed to ever say anything negative to anyone because it would, like, wound their fragile little ego?"

"And everyone made love and not war?" Ms. Lewinger asked, straight-faced. "I assure you, I'm being honest. You should think about making art your college major."

Joey smiled. "Thanks," she said softly. "Really. I—"

The classroom door opened. Aaron Poole. Male model. Fully dressed. But still.

Even though he now wore jeans and a white Boston College T-shirt, Joey imagined that she could still see every sinewy muscle and provocative bulge on his body.

"Aaron!" Ms. Lewinger called. "Come see this."

"Oh, no!" Joey cried, closing her sketch pad. Aaron came over to them. "Aaron, this is Joey Potter, one of the students who's been sketching you. Joey, Aaron."

"Yeah, we met briefly last week," Aaron said, nodding. "How's it going?"

"Fine," Joey mumbled. Her teeth stuck to her lips

as if she'd just chewed a big spoonful of crunchy Skippy.

"So, do I get to look at what you've done?" Aaron asked, grinning down at Joey.

What a face. What a smile. Her knees felt momentarily weak. "Oh, well, I, uh . . ."

Ms. Lewinger put her hand lightly on Joey's shoulder. "You can't be an artist without being brave, Joey."

Right. Joey took a deep breath. Slowly she opened her pad to her drawing of Aaron. If he was at all embarrassed to see himself depicted nearly naked on Joey's pad, he didn't show it. Which was fine, because Joey was embarrassed enough for the both of them.

If only he wasn't so incredibly gorgeous. Standing inches from him, she could feel the heat he gave off, and she could feel herself responding to it. Which was just so . . . icky. So not her. So . . . so *hormonal.*

"What did you say your name was again?" Aaron asked.

So Dawson had been right. The male model was a mental midget. Good. Then she could totally write him off.

"Joey," she said slowly, then separated the syllables for him. "Jo-ee."

"Well, Jo-ee," Aaron repeated easily, "I've been an artist's model since I was a sophomore in high school. I've seen a lot of drawings of me. And I have to say that yours is one of the best. Really."

"I told her it was excellent," Ms. Lewinger added.

"Oh." Oh? Joey winced. She couldn't believe that

she of the endless quips had just responded with "Oh."

"Thanks," she added, closing her pad and gathering up her stuff.

The teacher went over to her desk and busied herself with some paperwork. Aaron sat on the edge of Joey's desk. "Have you been drawing long?"

"For about the last hour," Joey mumbled, doing up the buckle on her backpack.

Aaron laughed. "Very literal. I meant have you been pursuing your art for very long?"

"It's a new thing for me," Joey admitted, still fiddling with her backpack buckle. "I saw this art exhibit, and . . . I don't know. I really love it, but . . ."

"Hey, you're allowed to finish your sentences."

Joey finally raised her eyes to meet his. "Gee, thanks for the permission. I've always wanted to completely finish them."

He pointed at her, his eyes dancing. "That was a split infinitive—a grammar no-no. I'm an English major."

"And I'm in a major hurry," Joey lied, throwing her backpack strap over her shoulder. "Nice splitting infinitives with you."

He laughed again. "And here I thought you were shy."

"And here I thought you were just a pretty, uh . . . face." She headed for the door, still looking at him. It was as if she could see right through his clothes. Muscles. Sinewy lines of masculine perfection that—

She bumped into the wall. Hard.

Ms. Lewinger was discreet enough to pretend not to notice. But Aaron laughed his loudest laugh yet.

"It just so happens that I did that on purpose," Joey explained, spitting a long strand of her hair out of her mouth. "Well, bye."

She rushed out of the art room, her face blazing red, an image of Aaron Poole stamped in her fevered mind.

And all the Lady Macbeth pronouncements of "Out, out, damned spot" couldn't seem to make him go away.

Chapter 7

Deputy Doug's beeper went off. He looked down at it.

"Someone got brought in on a DWI—driving while intoxicated," he told Dawson and Paccy. "I can tell from the code. Dawson, can you spot Pacey on these next sets? I have to go back to the stationhouse. Duty calls." He bolted up the stairs.

"Be gentle with that nightstick!" Pacey called after him in a falsetto.

Dawson looked at his watch. Seven-thirty. He wanted to be home by eight, because he'd taken Louis Malle's *Au Revoir les Enfants* home from ScreenPlay, the video store where he and Pacey worked part-time. It was the original version with subtitles. It had just come in with that day's mail delivery. Dawson wanted to be the first to see it.

"Well, you're not nearly as manly as Deputy

Doug, but you'll have to do," Pacey told Dawson. "Time to spot me on Monday night pecs."

"I have to admit, Pacey, I'm amazed that you're still doing this."

"Ha. And you thought you knew me."

"I do know you. What I don't know is why you're still obsessed with this bodybuilding idiocy. And please don't give me that insulting line about buff guys getting babes."

"All right, I won't," Pacey said smugly, sitting on the weight bench. "You can just *think* about it instead."

Dawson stepped behind the bench. "Has it occurred to you that you might have a persistent, harmful, and apparently escalating disease called body image obsession?"

"When I turn into Buff Boy, all manner of female pulchritude will be obsessed with my body. I'll have my pick. I don't call that a disease. I call that Nirvana."

"I thought you were doing all this to impress Andie."

"Andie who?"

"What, she dumped you?" Dawson asked.

"No, she didn't dump me. She just wants even more . . . space. I'm fine with it. I can feel myself radiate pheromones from my testosterone-filled body even as we speak."

"What do you know about pheromones?" Dawson asked.

"So I listened one day in biology, I had nothing else to do," Pacey admitted. "Soon the babes will be sniffing me out, Dawson. Hang around. You can choose amongst my leftovers." He positioned himself and pressed his hands against the barbell.

"You are deeply disturbed, Pacey."

"Thank you. Now, just spot the bar so I don't drop it on myself, and hold off on the speeches. Ready?"

Dawson nodded, and Pacey lifted the barbell straight up. He was pressing five pounds more than he had when he was starting out—not exactly Olympian progress, but still progress.

"Five . . . six . . . seven . . ." Pacey started to struggle with the barbell on the eighth rep, and Dawson positioned his hands in the middle to steady it.

"—and eight!" Pacey said, finishing the eighth rep, setting the barbell back down on its rack. "I'm telling you, Dawson, if you'd just have called me filthy worm or disgusting maggot or piece of rotting roadkill, I could have gotten two more reps out that set. I respond very well to negative reinforcement, seeing as I've heard so much of it in my life."

Dawson scrutinized Pacey. "What do you weigh now? Because you look thinner now than when you got started."

"I'm the same," Pacey admitted, still prone on the bench. "But it's just a matter of time before I bulk up." He grinned. "Are you thinking it?"

"To the buff go the babes, to the weenies go the woofers," Dawson groaned.

"What?" an outraged female voice demanded.

Dawson and Pacey both swung their heads toward the top of the basement stairs. Joey stood there, her hands on her hips. She was not a happy camper.

"Hi there," Pacey called. "Like my little motto? I'm thinking of having it tattooed on my manly biceps."

"You do that, Pacey. It will serve as fair warning to any girls delusional enough to think they might be interested in you." Joey came down the stairs. "How's everything down here in gym land?"

"How did you get in, anyhow?" Pacey asked.

"It was rugged," Joey replied, sitting on the step. "I rang the doorbell, no one answered, I tried the door, it was open. For the home of the chief of police and Deputy Doug, I wouldn't call that very security-conscious."

"Yeah, but wouldn't it be a thing of beauty to see that headline in the local newspaper?" Pacey mused. " 'Chief of police home robbery called easy pickings.' My father would give birth from the shame of it all. So, strip on down, Joey. Let's work up a sweat."

"With you?" Joey asked. "Gruesome thought. Actually, I wanted to talk to you about Andie."

Pacey stopped stretching. "Don't tell me—she asked you to tell me that she misses me more than summer vacation but she's afraid to admit it, right? The girl is crazed for me, I knew it."

"Well, it's a little more complicated," Joey hedged.

"You mean she really does want him back?" Dawson asked.

"I . . . can't discuss it with you, Dawson," Joey said.

Dawson shrugged. He knew it was stupid to feel left out, but he still did. Joey had come over to talk privately with Pacey. And he was heading home to a silent, empty house because his mom was working overtime at the station again. He thought about calling his dad. But he didn't want to look as pathetic as he felt.

Dawson looped his backpack over his shoulder. "Hey, Joey, I got *Au Revoir les Enfants*. Subtitles, popcorn, you up for it?"

"I really have to talk with Pacey," Joey said.

"Oh. Sure. Well, some other time. It's easier to concentrate on the more subtle nuances of the film when I'm alone, anyway." Dawson left the two of them in the basement. A truly terrifying thought came over him. Could Joey be interested in Pacey? No, that was ludicrous. Most of the time, Joey barely tolerated Pacey.

To the buff go the . . .

"Shut up, Dawson," he told himself as he headed to the door. "Just shut up."

Pacey put his hands behind his head and leaned them against the wall. "Okay, tell me what my lady said, word for word."

"Nothing," Joey replied.

"Run that by me again?"

"Nothing," Joey repeated. "As in zero, silence, *nada.*"

Pacey sat up. "I seem to be missing something here. You told me that Andie told you—"

"I lied."

"You lied. Meaning Andie didn't tell you anything." Joey nodded.

"Meaning Andie and I are still wherever it is that Andie and I are."

"I'm impressed with your mental faculties," Joey said.

"Last I heard, you and Andie are free agents who are still dating, sort of, but you can see other people."

Pacey nodded. "Ah, it's all so clear to me now."

"Which is why it's okay for you to pretend to be my boyfriend."

Pacey threw his arms around Joey. "You'd do that for me, just to make Andie jealous? What a woman, what a friend, what a—"

"Crock," Joey filled in, extricating herself from his sloppy embrace. "I'm asking if you'll do me a favor. I need you to pretend to be my boyfriend Wednesday afternoon. After that, you can go back to being . . . whatever you are."

"Buff Boy, thank you very much," Pacey said. "I have a feeling my line here is: 'Why do you want me to pretend to be your boyfriend, Joey?'"

"Because I'm going on an interview Wednesday afternoon for a modeling job because it's the only way I can think of to make enough money to save the Ice House, and I don't want to go alone, and I don't want to ask a girl to come with me in case the guy who interviews me is like that photographer in *Fame*—you know, the slime-lizard guy who talks her into taking off her shirt—so I thought I'd ask you to come with me and pretend to be my boyfriend. And if you say one nasty thing about the humor involved in my going to a modeling interview, I will personally make sure that the ability to have children is no longer an option in your future."

Pacey scratched his chin. "You. Modeling, huh?"

"If you smirk, I swear I'll—"

Pacey held his hand up. "I am smirkless. In fact, I'm seeing a big future for you. You'll become a supermodel and go by one name: Joee, with some kind of a fancy French vowel thing going on. I'll manage you. You'll introduce me to your supermodel friends—"

"All I'm asking for is one afternoon, Pacey," Joey interrupted. "Yes or no?"

He cocked his head at her. "Why me?"

"Who was I supposed to ask, Dawson? Can you even picture that little scenario?"

"I see your point. The answer to your question, Jo-ee," he said, pronouncing the *J* as in *bonjour*, "is yes. I buff enough now to mingle wiz ze be-yoo-tee-ful pee-pull." Pacey got up and stretched, checking out his reflection in the floor-to-ceiling mirror.

"One other thing," Joey said as she got up, too. "You absolutely, positively cannot tell a single soul about this. I'm trusting you, Pacey."

"Agreed."

She waited, assuming a more teasing comeback would follow, but Pacey didn't say another word.

"Thanks, Pacey. Really."

"You're welcome," he replied. "Really."

She looked at him skeptically. "How come you're acting normal? It's very disconcerting."

"The still waters of Pacey Witter run deep," he replied. Then he went back to his workout.

Joey watched him for a minute, then she went upstairs and let herself out. Well, she had the appointment. She had the fake boyfriend. She was going for it.

She really didn't have a choice. Or else it was good-bye, Ice House. And on to a future that was too scary to contemplate.

Chapter 8

As the bus they were on pulled into the Falmouth station, Pacey eyed Joey critically as she stared out the window and nervously bit a cuticle. She wore exactly what she'd worn to school that day—jeans, a T-shirt, and a red sweater with too long sleeves. Per usual, she had on only the barest touch of eye makeup and some raspberry lipstick, and her hair was carelessly tied back with a leather shoestring from an old pair of work boots.

"Correct me if I'm wrong," Pacey said, "but aren't models supposed to look . . . modelish?"

Joey fixed him with a deadly look. "What is that supposed to mean?"

"You know, hair mussed to perfection, perky bare breasts that just happen to show through the—"

"My hair is permanently mussed, Pacey, and from the neck down I suggest you think of me as Neuter Girl."

He draped an arm across her shoulders. "But you're my girlfriend."

Joey lifted his arm as if it were a dead carp. "Please don't feel that you have to take your role seriously on my account." She dropped his arm into his lap.

"Falmouth Station," the bus driver said, opening the door. Pacey and Joey got off the bus. Joey checked her watch. Her go-see (Jen had explained that that's what a modeling interview was called) was scheduled for five o'clock at the Falmouth Inn, and it was already a quarter to five. But the person she'd spoken with on the phone had told her it was only a five-minute walk from the bus station.

Jocy took out the directions she'd scribbled down. "This way two blocks to Dover Street," she said, "then right on Main Street, and we should see the Falmouth Inn."

"Listen, just out of curiosity, why would a legit modeling job look for models in Falmouth?" Pacey asked as they walked quickly down the street.

"They hold these things all over the country, is what they told me," Joey explained. "To look for new faces."

"Sounds highly suspicious."

"So we'll scope it out," Jocy said.

"You sure you want to do this?"

"No. But Bessie's new job cooking at World O' Pancakes is not going to get us the Ice House back. The next street should be Main Street."

"What if they rip you off, Joey?"

"They won't."

"What if they do?"

Joey turned to him. "Are you here to help me?" she asked archly. "Because if it's discouragement I need, I can just call Dawson."

Pacey held up his right hand. "Scout's honor, Buff Boy is here to help—"

"Thank you."

"—and to meet some incredible-looking babes," he added.

They easily found the Falmouth Inn and went into the small, elegant lobby. Classical music played softly. Everything looked tasteful—from the crystal bowl of polished red apples on a mahogany table to the Ralph Lauren–clad guests.

Joey's eyes slid over to Pacey, in his baggy jeans and trying-too-hard sunglasses, then she looked down at her own school-girl jeans and sneakers. She wanted to run out the door and drag Pacey with her. The idea that she was about to interview for a job as a model seemed like the dumbest idea in the history of dumb ideas.

Pacey nudged her shoulder and cocked his head toward a small sign: LA PETITE LIZ BETTE GO-SEE, MODELS BY APPT. ONLY, CONFERENCE SUITE 101. An arrow pointed to a corridor to the right.

"That's it," Joey said, her hands growing clammy. Resolutely, she headed down the corridor, Pacey at her side.

Joey pushed the door open to the conference suite. Inside it looked like an unremarkable living-room; the only thing that differentiated it from any other hotel living room suite was the folding chairs that had been set up around the room to augment the beige couch and beige wing chair. Every flat surface was covered with a sitting, perching, or leaning girl. Each seemed to have some sort of portfolio with her. They were all perfectly made-up, perfectly coiffed, and dressed in sexy clothes that showed off their perfect bodies.

Before Joey could even think about what she was doing, instinct took over. She opened the door and fled.

Pacey ran out after her. "What is this sudden urge to run the hundred-meter dash?" he called out.

"I can't do this, this was stupid, let's just go." They were in the lobby, Joey heading for the door to the street.

Pacey lunged for her arm. "Hey!" He spun her around. "Don't wimp out now."

"Did you see those girls in there? Did you?" Joey demanded. "They look like the girls in Capeside who whisper about Joey Potter and her messed-up family and her messed-up life. Willingly subjecting myself to that kind of humiliation borders on the psychotic, and I am merely neurotic, so let's go."

"You sure?"

Joey folded her arms. "I'm sure."

Pacey stuffed his hands in the pockets of his jeans. "Because the thing is, Joey, I think you can do this."

"Right."

"No, I mean I *really* think you can do this. Model. Get the gig."

Joey pushed some stray hair off her face. "Wait, are you in sensitive pretend-boyfriend mode now?"

"Pretty much," Pacey agreed.

"It's failing."

"Okay, how about this, then. The hot momma who wants me desperately might be sitting in that suite this very minute, and your selfishness will have deprived me of empty and meaningless sexual ecstasy beyond my wildest dreams."

The corners of Joey's mouth edged up into a smile.

"Ah, your face is having a Mona Lisa moment."

Joey laughed. "You have occasional lapses into decency, Pacey."

"Buff *and* sensitive, I would definitely go for me," Pacey decided. "Now, what say we head back in there and show them just what the bottom fish of Capeside are made of?"

They retraced their steps back to Suite 101. This time when they went in, Joey noticed a very thin woman in her thirties sitting behind a small desk. She had cropped bright red hair and wore a black T-shirt and black jeans. She looked up and eyed Joey coolly.

"Hi," Joey said, walking over to the desk. "I'm—"

"Fill zis out," the woman said with a French accent, pushing a clipboard with a form on it toward Joey. "Give it to me when you are done. You are number forty-eight. Alanzo iz now on number twenty-nine."

There was no place left to sit, so Joey sat on the floor leaning against the wall, Pacey next to her. The form was basic—name, address, phone number. Joey stopped when she got to age and nibbled on the end of the pen. Eighteen, she wrote in, just in case.

After that, it asked her measurements and sizes

and modeling experience. Since she didn't know her measurements and had no modeling experience, this took five seconds. She took the form back up to the woman behind the desk, who didn't even bother to look up from the edition of *Paris Match* magazine she was reading.

Joey and Pacey went back to sit against the wall. Every few minutes, one of the gorgeous girls went into the next room. When one came out, the woman behind the desk would call out the next number.

"They're sure not in there for very long," Joey said nervously as a short, curvy girl with a blond bob exited the interview.

"Maybe I should go comfort her," Pacey said, watching the girl leave.

Other girls went in for their interviews, and other girls arrived to fill out forms and wait. Joey got more and more nervous. After what felt like forever, the woman behind the desk called out, "Forty-eight."

"That's me!" Joey jumped up, tripping on her own feet. Fortunately, she didn't actually fall over.

"How nice for you," the French woman said dryly, cocking her head toward the door. Joey and Pacey headed for it.

"Young man, where do you seenk you are goink?" the woman called to Pacey.

"I'm accompanying my girlfriend," Pacey said, nodding seriously. "I always accompany her on these . . .uh . . ."

"Go-sees," Joey hissed in his ear.

"Go-sees," Pacey said.

"Not on zis one," the woman said. "Do you see any uhzer boyfriends in zis rhoom?"

Pacey had to admit he didn't.

"Zen why don't you have a seat? Your girlfriend will be out in just a few moments, just like ze forty-seven girls we see before her today and ze fifty-seven we see yesterday. None have experienced ze bodily injury, no?"

Embarrassed, Pacey sat down as Joey took a deep breath and went in. It looked like a hotel bedroom, except there was no bed. A silver-haired man in his fifties was sitting at a desk, and there was a folding chair in front of him.

"Come in." He waved distractedly as he pawed through a huge pile of model photos heaped on the desk. He never looked up. "Sit down, be with you in a minute."

Joey sat, nervously biting her lower lip.

"Ah, found her!" The man snagged a photo from the pile and picked up the phone, punching a button. "Yeah, Véronique, I found the girl who did the shoot for Hothouse Bikinis . . . well, that's one, anyway . . . no, you can call her later." He hung up, then he finally looked up at Joey. "I'm Alanzo Bartkevicius. Call me Alan." He held out his hand.

Joey had no idea what she was supposed to do, so she just sat there.

"Your form?"

"Oh. Right." Reddening, she handed him her form.

He scanned it. "Joey Potter," he read. "Joey is short for—?"

She'd been down this road before. She loathed and detested her given name, Josephine, and had even lied to a cute guy she'd met in New York and said her name was Joelle.

But something stubborn made her decide to tell the truth now. What the heck, it wasn't like she had a shot, anyway. "Josephine," she said, holding her chin a little higher.

He smiled. "That was my mom's name. Great lady. So, let's take a look at your book, Josephine."

"Excuse me?"

"Your portfolio," he said. "Modeling photos?"

"Er . . . I forgot my portfolio today," she invented.

"Meaning you don't have one. What modeling have you done?"

"Uh . . . some," Joey said.

He raised his eyebrows.

"Okay, none," Joey admitted defiantly. "Unless you count my stellar performance as runner-up to Miss Windjammer."

"Miss *who?*"

Joey stood up. "Forget it. Sorry I wasted your time."

She was halfway to the door when he commanded, "Stop!" She did, and turned around slowly.

He smiled. "I see you can follow directions, Josephine. That's a beginning. There's some outfits in the bathroom. Go try one on."

Joey gawked at him.

He sighed. "This is a go-see for a catalog shoot. I need girls who fit into the outfits. And I can't very well tell if you fit into the outfits unless you try on the outfits."

She hesitated. "This is legit, right?"

"As legit as modeling gets, anyway," Alan said. "I held go-sees in New York, Atlanta, Chicago, and Miami before this one, all because the owner of this French catalog has a thing for fresh American faces. Who am I to quibble?"

"It's just that . . . you know, you hear a lot about . . . things," Joey said lamely.

"Look, dear, I'm certainly not hitting on you. For one thing, I'm gay. And for another thing . . . well, I'm still gay. Now, do you want me to consider you for this booking or not?"

"Yes, I do," Joey said.

"Fine." He pointed to a door. "And dress quickly, or I'll have to move on."

Joey almost ran into the bathroom. On the shower curtain hung a dozen outfits.

They were all lingerie. Very skimpy lingerie.

She stuck her head out of the bathroom. "Uh, excuse me!" she called.

"What?"

"This is all lingerie."

"That would probably be because La Petite Liz Bette is a French lingerie line."

"Well, no one told me that."

"Well, now someone has. You have ninety seconds, Josephine."

Joey closed the door, swallowed hard, and picked out one of the few outfits that wasn't transparent— black silk bikini panties with an over layer of red chiffon and a matching camisole that tied with red ribbons.

"Think bathing suit, Joey," she mumbled to herself. "Your bathing suit shows a lot more flesh than this outfit."

She marched into the room and stood in front of Alan, her arms folded over her breasts.

"That pose is delightfully butch, but it doesn't exactly sell the outfit," Alan pointed out dryly.

Joey reluctantly dropped her arms. Alan grabbed something from the desk and headed for her.

"What?" She jumped back.

"It's a tape measure." He held it up. "You didn't give me your measurements."

Joey still looked doubtful.

Alan sighed. "I must be losing my mind." He thrust the tape measure at her. "Take them yourself."

Joey quickly took her measurements and read them off to Alan.

"Fine. You can go change," he said.

"That's it?"

He rubbed the space between his eyes. "Call me psychic, but I have this feeling that you are a young model without a great deal of experience. Your phone number is on your form. And there is a reason for that."

"Meaning don't call us, we'll call you," Joey translated.

"Excellent deduction," Alan said, leafing through his photos again.

He didn't even bother to look up when Joey left.

Chapter 9

Later that night, Joey was home baby-sitting, as Bessie had gotten a one-night gig bartending at a private party. She had been doing a little shading on her drawing of Aaron Poole but mostly was thinking about Dawson and everything he'd said about how shallow it was to judge people on the basis of looks.

She turned to a clean sheet of paper, where she began to draw Dawson from memory. It was always so easy for her to draw him. Maybe it was because she knew every plane of his face, every line of his torso—no model was necessary. Time fell away; she kept drawing. She lingered over the shading of his cheekbones, the outline of his lips, his eyes, his—

Through her open window, she heard the characteristic *swish-swish* of oars entering water. Someone was paddling across the creek.

Dawson. She looked down at her drawing. It was almost as if she had willed him to come to her. But why would I do that, she asked herself, when I was the one who wanted to see other people?

Best friend. The words whispered in her brain. Best friend. You miss your best friend.

That had to be it. She quickly shut her sketchbook and went to her window, picking up the high-powered flashlight that she kept on her bookshelf. She shined it out into the creek. It was Dawson. Happiness filled her.

Until she realized that he wasn't alone.

Jen. Jen and Dawson in Dawson's boat.

Joey grabbed a sweatshirt and waited on the porch as Dawson tied up the boat. It was an unusually warm spring night, the air fresh with the promise of renewal.

Dawson and Joey? Dawson and Jen? Joey wondered.

"So, what brings the two of you to the seedy side of the creek?" Joey asked brightly as they reached the house.

Jen and Dawson looked at each other uncomfortably.

"We have something for you," Jen said. "To help."

Joey raised her eyebrows.

Dawson reached in his pocket and took out an envelope. He handed it to Joey, who opened it.

Inside were five crisp hundred-dollar bills.

Joey handed it right back to him. "Forget it, Dawson. However good your intentions, I can't take this."

"But we want you to use it for the Ice House," he said.

"I gathered that, but I won't take it."

"Look," Jen began, "there's no reason to let pride stand in the way of—"

"Charity?" Joey asked pointedly.

"Friendship," Jen said. "I was going to say friendship."

Dawson took Joey's hand, gently put the money back in it, and held it. "It's a loan, Joey. I can't take it back. What you see there is a Topps 1957 near-mint-condition Sandy Koufax baseball card—"

"—plus a pair of diamond stud earrings that my mother gave me as a bribe to keep my mouth shut about one of her less sterling escapades," Jen added. "Believe me, pawning them was my idea of a good time."

Dawson still held Joey's hand. He gently closed her fingers around the money.

She couldn't look at either of them. "Since when do you collect baseball cards, Dawson?"

"My dad gave me a couple the year I started and ended my Little League career. I spent the entire season hitless, and then in the last game the pitcher threw me a fastball that broke my nose."

Joey smiled softly. "I remember that. It wasn't exactly a *Field of Dreams* moment." She handed the money back to him. "Thanks. Both of you. But I can't accept it."

"Joey—" Dawson began.

"I just can't," she insisted. "Anyway, five hundred dollars would hardly put a dent in how much money we need."

Jen kicked at the porch railing base with her foot. "Have you thought any more about that job I told you about?"

"What job?" Dawson asked.

"Nothing," Joey said quickly. "Forget it."

"I saw an ad in the Sunday paper about a modeling gig that I thought Joey would be perfect for," Jen said.

Dawson chuckled. "Seriously, what was it?"

Joey turned on him. "What do you mean, *seriously?* I could model!"

"Contrary to your classic overreaction, Joey, I wasn't laughing at the idea of your being a model," Dawson explained. "I was laughing at the idea that you'd believe a legitimate modeling job would advertise in the newspaper, as if it was a waitressing gig or something."

Joey's chin jutted out. "A gig with which I am well familiar. Look, I know this is difficult for your well-fed mind to grasp, Dawson, but when you're broke, the idea of finding a modeling job in the newspaper does not seem particularly far-fetched."

"I'm sure Kate Moss checks the want ads on a regular basis," Dawson teased.

"Give it a rest, Dawson," Jen said. "Some of my friends in New York got legit modeling gigs through the newspaper. It's not impossible."

"But it is impossibly shallow," Dawson said.

"As opposed to my current deep, high-paying career as a waitress?" Joey asked sarcastically.

"Look, if Joey was willing to enter the Miss Capeside pageant to make money, why shouldn't she try to model?" Jen asked. "It's no more exploitive than beauty pageants."

"I could have sworn the root word 'exploit' was in that sentence," Dawson pointed out.

"So were the words 'make money,' Dawson," Jen shot back. "Looks and money make America go 'round. We all buy into it, so there's no point in pretending we don't."

"Well, I don't," Dawson said. "And Joey doesn't, either." He looked over at Joey for confirmation, but she was suddenly busy studying her sneakers.

Jen tapped Dawson on the shoulder. "When you kissed me," she said, her voice low and sexy, "was it because of my high IQ?"

Dawson took an uneasy step away from her.

"And when you kissed Joey," Jen went on, "was it because she does volunteer work? I mean, those things are so attractive to you, Dawson, and looks are meaningless, right?"

Now both girls were staring at him, waiting.

"Attraction is an ephemeral, abstract thing," Dawson began. "To reduce someone to the sum of their physical parts is to exclude what makes them essentially . . . them."

The girls looked at each other. "He's full of it," they both said at once.

Dawson spread his arms wide. "This is ridiculous! Would you rather I be like Pacey and slobber over a girl just because she has a certain body type? Is that what you really want?"

"Personally, I was thinking more along the lines of honesty," Jen said. "Just admit that it's the physical that gets you first, and everything else is secondary."

"I can't admit that because it isn't true," Dawson insisted, "any more than it's true that Joey would debase herself by selling her looks. I mean, looks, body, what's the difference, really?"

"Look, I'm not modeling, okay?" Joey said. She knew she was never going to get the catalog job, so what difference did a little lie make? Suddenly, she was sick of the conversation and really exhausted. "I have to get going."

"I'm holding this money for you, Joey," Dawson said. "You just say the word at any time."

"Right," Jen agreed. "It's yours." They headed for the creek.

They climbed back into the boat, and Joey headed back to the house. It was so shabby-looking. The thin carpeting in the living room was ripped, and there was a purple stain where the baby had spilled grape juice. The springs were coming out on one side of the sofa, and a bookcase was held up by bricks underneath it.

Joey remembered how this room had looked when she was a kid. They didn't have much money, but her mom had made everything beautiful with little scarves, a coat of paint, a welcoming bowl of fruit.

Sudden tears came to Joey's eyes, and she willed them away. That was then, this was now. And if she didn't figure out some way to save the Ice House, she and Bessie could lose even this home, sweet home.

She went into the kitchen for some water and

noticed that the light was blinking on the answering machine.

One flash. One message.

Joey pressed "play" and waited for the tape to rewind.

"Zis message iz for Josephine, yes?" a female French-accented voice said. "Zis is Véronique, Alanzo Bartkevicius's assistant. I am ringing to say Alan has selected you for ze La Petite Liz Bette catalog shoot planned for zis Friday in Boston. Please call to confirm." A number followed.

Joey just stood there, too numb to move. Then she played the message again, to make sure that it wasn't Pacey playing a trick on her.

It wasn't. The message was real.

Joey—correction, *Josephine*—was going to be a model.

Chapter 10

Nervous did not begin to cover it.

Joey looked out the window of the bus and said a little prayer to whatever gods had deemed Friday an inservice day at school for teachers. Which meant classes were canceled. Which meant freedom to take the modeling job without cutting classes. One of Bessie's friends had agreed to watch Alexander while Bessie did a three-day convention catering gig in Boston, and the way Joey figured it, she'd be home long before Bessie would realize she'd been far away from Capeside.

In Boston. A snort of nervous laughter escaped from Joey's lips. It would be just her luck to run into her sister in Boston.

Next to her, Pacey yawned loudly. "I hope you realize that I expect a little something from my girlfriend in return for getting me on a bus this early in the morning," he said.

"How about a knee to the family jewels?" Joey suggested sweetly.

"Family jewels, what a lovely expression," Pacey mused. "That would make my father's the chief family jewels, and Deputy Doug's the gay family jewels, and—"

"You are so not on a roll," Joey told him.

The bus pulled into the depot in Boston, and Joey practically pulled Pacey off the bus. Véronique had said to be at the loft for the shoot at seven sharp, to have her hair and makeup done. It was already six forty-five.

Darting through the crowded bus station, they made their way to the taxi stand and jumped into the first available cab. The driver nodded when Joey gave him the address, and he pulled out into traffic.

"Véronique said it's only a five-minute taxi ride," Joey said nervously. She took out a piece of bubble gum and unwrapped it, popped it into her mouth, and chewed furiously.

"Hey, you're cool, Josephine," Pacey told her, slipping on his sunglasses. "Buff Man is at your side."

"What happened to Buff Boy?"

He smiled smugly. "I've graduated."

As it was pre-rush hour, the traffic was light, and within five minutes the taxi pulled up in front of a nondescript gray, deserted-looking building.

"This is it?" Joey asked uncertainly, getting out of the cab.

"This is the address you gave me," the driver said.

Joey paid him, and she and Pacey went into the

building. Someone had taped a small sign on the wall: LA PETITE LIZ BETTE SHOOT, FIFTH FLOOR LOFT. They took the elevator up. The elevator doors opened on a huge room in the midst of organized chaos. Three young women, carrying clipboards, were going through racks of lingerie, checking them off and marking which outfit was for which model, then rolling each rack into a freight elevator. Along one wall were makeup mirrors, brightly lit, and high canvas director stools. As soon as Véronique saw Joey, she hurried over.

"Josephine, correct? You are late!" she scolded.

"But you said seven—"

"I said six exactly," Véronique insisted, "for ze hair and ze makeup. Ze ozers have already gone!"

"Gone where?" Joey asked, bewildered.

"To ze shoot, to ze shoot! I explain all of zis to you on ze phone, no?"

"No," Joey said. "I thought the shoot was—"

"We wait now only for Renaldo, but he iz always late, we meet him downstairs at ze van." She stabbed the button for the elevator, and her eyes fixed on Pacey. "Ah, ze boyfriend."

"Excuse me," Joey said, "but where is it that we're—"

"Does ze boyfriend have a name?" Véronique asked.

"Ze boyfriend does," Pacey assured her. "Pacey."

"Zis iz a name I haf never heard. Does it come wiz a last name?"

Pacey nodded. "Pacey . . . Buffman."

"Well, how nice of you to join us, Meester Buffman," Véronique said, pronouncing it "Boofman."

"Where are we going?" Joey asked loudly.

Véronique turned to her and shook her head. "You have forgotten? Zis is not professional."

"I didn't forget. I wasn't told!"

Véronique *tsk*ed, as if Joey were a wayward child. They got on the elevator. "So, I repeat it all to you. We do ze shoot at ze rented mansion, right outside of Boston. Alan, ze photographer, and ze crew have been zere since yesterday, setting up." She looked at her watch. "I am done with Renaldo!"

They walked out in front of the building. The lingerie was being loaded into a small truck, and a passenger van had arrived, its motor idling. Clearly it was waiting for them.

"Aren't I supposed to get made up or something?" Joey asked meekly.

"Ze makeup and hair arteests have gone already to ze site," Véronique explained, exasperated. "You are late!"

Joey decided it was pointless to protest her innocence again.

"Zay will do you when we get zere," Véronique said. She looked at her watch again. "I will kill Renaldo zis time, I cannot take zis! So, we get on ze van. Go, go, go!" She shooed Joey and Pacey in front of her.

They scrambled onto the van and took seats.

"Someone throw the woman some kava-kava," Pacey muttered to Joey.

"Kava what?" Joey asked.

"Herbal chill pill," Pacey translated. "Whoa, I think the infamous Renaldo has just rolled up."

Joey looked out the van window. A great-looking

guy in his early twenties jumped out of an Italian sports car, driven by a gorgeous blonde. He climbed into the van and took off his sunglasses. His features were perfectly chiseled, his hair dark, his eyes a startling blue. His jeans were worn to perfection, and the T-shirt under his leather jacket clung to the most perfectly defined torso Joey had ever seen.

"I may need to spend a tad more time in the gym," Pacey mused, eyeing Renaldo.

"Renaldo!" Véronique cried, throwing her arms around him. "You are a very bad boy for being so late!" She kissed him on one cheek, then the other, then they both sat down.

"Go, go, go!" she told the driver, waving her hand.

"Real people don't look like him," Pacey decided, eyeing Renaldo. "He's probably the sad, insecure product of massive plastic surgery."

"Dream on, Buffman," Joey said.

"Do you think that's what Andie wants?" Pacey asked.

"To my knowledge, Andie McPhee doesn't know ol' Renaldo over there," Joey said.

"What's to know? When you look like that, you can have the personality of a beer belch."

"Colorfully put," Joey allowed. "False but colorful."

"Right, like you wouldn't get jiggy with Renaldo."

"One of the many things that Andie and I have in common, besides a general desire to promote a great deal of space between you and us, Pacey, is that neither of us knows Renaldo, which kind of lets out the getting jiggy thing."

"To the buff—" Pacey began.

"Go the babes," Joey finished sourly. "You can't imagine how much that expression annoys me."

Pacey stretched and locked his fingers behind his neck. "Ah, but I can." He smirked.

Renaldo had gotten up, and now he took a seat across from them.

"Hey, I'm Renaldo." He held out his hand to Pacey.

"We heard," Pacey said, and gave Renaldo his most manly handshake. His voice got discernibly lower. "This is my lady, Josephine."

Joey shot Pacey a murderous look, which he blithely ignored.

"So, Josephine, you doing this gig?" Renaldo asked.

She shook her head yes and waited for him to laugh.

He didn't.

"Cool," is what he said.

"Listen, Renaldo, my man," Pacey said, leaning into the aisle. "I see by your cut that you train. Me, too—but then, I guess that's obvious."

Joey sank down lower in her seat, beyond humiliated.

"So," Pacey went on, "when you get a free mo' during the shoot, we'll talk bodybuilding in a big way."

"Whoa, serious *Gone With the Wind* moment," Joey said, staring out the van window as they pulled up to the mansion. It was red brick, with white pillars spaced along the stately porch, surrounded by acres of lush, manicured lawns. Recreational vehicles stood everywhere. The racks of lingerie were now being moved into the various vehicles. Dozens of people scurried around; a few stood outside the catering truck near a portable buffet table, sipping coffee.

"Go, go, go!" Véronique cried, shooing them out of the van. "Renaldo, you and ze ozer guy are in trailer two over zere. Angie iz doing your makeup. Ze outfits are in zere wiz ze assistahnt."

Renaldo saluted Véronique and took off before she could encourage him to go, go, go again.

Véronique turned to Joey. "You go to ze makeup and hair trailer, over zere." She looked at Pacey. "Meester Boofman, zere are folding chairs over zere under ze trees. Sit. Don't move."

"Sit. Don't move," Pacey repeated. "Consider it done." He caught Joey's eye and gave her a quick thumbs-up before sauntering away.

Joey hurried to the makeup van and went in. This was more makeshift than the makeup area back at the loft. There were three canvas director chairs with tall gooseneck lamps focused brightly on them, and a large card table that held a big black box full of cosmetics. Next to that was another table covered with hair-care products. Two full-length mirrors leaned against the side of the trailer.

Two young women stood by the director chairs. Each was sipping coffee and reading the morning paper. One had freckles and bright red hair messily caught on top of her head with chopsticks, the other was African-American with almond-shaped eyes and closely cut cropped hair.

"Hi," Joey said meekly. "I'm the model." She felt like a fraud just saying the words.

"Great, we've been waiting for you," the redhead said, jumping out of the chair. "Sit."

Joey did.

"It's Josephine, right? I'm Dani, that's Phoebe. I'm hair, she's makeup." She picked up some of Joey's hair and rubbed it between her fingers. "Great hair. We can do major lush with some hot rollers."

Phoebe scrutinized Joey's face. "What's with those eyebrows?"

"What?" Joey asked nervously.

"Don't you wax?" Phoebe asked, incredulous.

"No," Joey replied honestly.

Phoebe sighed. "Well, I'll have to pluck, then." She picked up dangerous-looking tweezers.

"No, my . . . modeling people like my eyebrows natural," Joey invented quickly.

"How Brooke Shields," Phoebe sneered, but she put the tweezers down. "It just really bites my butt when these agencies try to tell me how to do my job."

Dani began rolling Joey's long hair on large hot rollers, while Phoebe dotted her face with thick, creamy makeup base, then patted it in with a triangular sponge. A dazzling array of cosmetics followed—concealer, loose powder, eye shadows and liners and mascara, three different blushes, lip liner, lipstick, and lip gloss. Joey just sat there while her face was painted, her scalp growing hot from the rollers. She couldn't see how she looked because she wasn't facing the mirror, but no one seemed to care what she thought, anyway.

"Okay, do her, and then I'll touch her up," Phoebe told Dani, moving away.

Dani began deftly to unroll Joey's hair. Then she used gel and spray and a curling iron. After that, Phoebe powdered Joey's face again. Then they both stood scrutinizing her.

"Yeah?" Phoebe asked Dani.

"Yeah." Dani nodded. "Damn, we're good."

Before Joey could even turn around to check out her reflection in the mirror, they had hustled her out of the trailer and into the next trailer to get into her first outfit.

"You're Josephine, right? I'm Laura," a petite, Asian-featured young woman said, pawing through the wardrobe rack. "Per usual, the Dani and Phoebe show has put us behind schedule." She turned around to look at Joey, who was just standing there. "Well, hurry up and strip, we are so late."

Nervously, Joey slipped off her jeans, T-shirt, and sweater, standing there in her underwear, feeling like an idiot.

"There's a robe for you on the chair," Laura called, still going through the outfits. "Take everything off."

You need the money, you need the money, Joey chanted to herself as she pulled the luxurious terry-cloth robe on and then slipped her underwear off underneath it.

"Some rocket scientist numbered your outfits wrong," Laura said. She held out a hot-pink velvet bra and matching hot-pink velvet bikini panties. "Here."

"Th-this?" Joey stammered.

"Yeah, I know, who wants to put on velvet when it's so hot under those lights? But it's a winter catalog. And for pity's sake, hurry, before Véronique comes in here having one of her patented Parisian hissy fits."

Joey turned her back to Laura and fumbled into the outfit, then she quickly wrapped herself back in the robe.

"Okay, get down to the porch, they're waiting for you," Laura said. "Candi and Kim will detail you when you get there."

Detail, Joey thought, on the verge of hysteria. Like a car. She was about to step out of the trailer when she realized that she hadn't seen herself since the beginning of her transformation. She turned to the floor-length mirror and opened her robe.

Bizarre. Some other girl was standing there, not her.

This girl's hair was pouffy, curly, and wavy, and her face was so covered with cosmetics she didn't even recognize herself. The only giveaway was that below the truly stupid pink velvet underwear were her own scuffed-up sneakers on her own big feet.

Joey hurried to the front porch, which was full of people. She saw Pacey, who waved at her.

Three other female models were already there, with various people fussing over their hair, makeup, and outfits as techies adjusted the huge klieg lights on them. They all introduced themselves to Joey. There was Sloan Johnson, who looked like Cameron Diaz with longer hair and bigger breasts; Belva, six feet tall and African-American, with unbelievable muscle tone—someone was fastening a fake ponytail to the back of her head; and Royce, who had huge green eyes and long, jet-black, perfectly straight hair.

"Joey," she managed, but just barely. Her mouth wasn't working. She tried to smile. That didn't work, either.

"Ouch! I have a scalp with nerve endings on it, you know!" Belva yelled at the young woman pinning the ponytail to her head.

"Find pink slippers that fit," a young man told Joey, cocking his head toward a huge table that held satin slippers, feather boas, and various props. Joey found some pink slippers and changed into them. Then she stood on the porch feeling like an idiot and an imposter, while the other models chatted easily with each other.

Renaldo walked over to them. He was naked except for a pair of cherry-red silk boxer shorts.

"Renaldo! I didn't know you were doing this shoot," Royce squealed, giving Renaldo a kiss.

"Please, I just redid your lips, no kissing!" someone instructed.

Véronique hurried over to them. "Where's A.P.?"

"There was some kind of mixup about which outfit was first, and he—" Renaldo began. "Oh, wait, here he comes."

The door to the guys' trailer swung open, and another male model in a bathrobe stepped down.

Joey's jaw dropped open. Walking toward her, looking beyond perfect, wearing a black silk robe and black silk pajama bottoms, was the model from her Advanced Life Drawing class, Aaron Poole.

Chapter 11

"**S**hot thirty-five, this is shot thirty-five," another of the seemingly endless supply of assistants called out through a megaphone. "Josephine and Renaldo, to the second-floor bedroom."

It was already two-thirty in the afternoon. Joey was standing with Pacey near the catering truck, eating a tuna sandwich. It was amazing how quickly she'd gotten used to having her picture taken wearing skimpy lingerie.

Actually, most of it hadn't been very skimpy. And everyone had been comfortable and professional, and so far, luckily, her outfits had been the least skimpy of all the models. She'd simply copied the things they did and the way they posed. Loud rock music played, which made it easier to move into different poses, and the photographers and their assistants were all very encouraging.

In order to accomplish the herculean task of shooting the entire catalog in one day, there were three photographers working simultaneously in various parts of the house. So far, Joey hadn't been in any shots with the guys, and she hadn't seen Aaron since first thing that morning.

She'd modeled six outfits so far. In two of them she wore velvet underwear, as did Sloan, and both pretended to be flipping pancakes in the kitchen. Then she'd worn a red velvet and satin robe and snuggled up in a swing on the porch; then she wore a gorgeous black silk gown and matching robe in the opulent living room, where she and Royce were supposed to be opening Christmas presents. And, finally, all the female models had worn babydolls and pretended to be having a pillow fight, feathers flying through the air.

Sometimes her hair was pinned up, sometimes it was all put over one shoulder. Her lipstick was changed with each outfit, her makeup freshened up. Assistants would bring her water or juice—she was treated as if she was important and gorgeous.

And . . . well, the truth was, it was fun.

"Josephine and Renaldo, hold for five, we've had a klieg blow up here," the voice said over the megaphone.

"Good, I can keep eating," Joey said, reaching for a doughnut. "I'm starving."

"Better watch it, Josephine," Pacey said as he sipped a Coke. "See-through undies show every pound."

"May I point out that I haven't modeled any see-through undies?" Joey replied.

"Sloan has." Pacey put his hand over his heart. "Baby-blue lace and this sheer stuff. She walked by. I fell in love."

"That's deep, Pacey."

"Our eyes met," Pacey went on. "It was Kismet."

"She spoke to you?" Joey asked.

"Words weren't necessary."

Joey grabbed his Coke and took a swallow, then handed it back to him. "Dream on, Buffman. Gotta run."

"Give Sloan my best!" Pacey called.

Joey turned back to him. "That is a frightening thought."

"Up the stairs, the bedroom on the right," an assistant with a clipboard told Joey.

Joey went into the bedroom. It was gorgeous—a large canopy bed was centered on a tapestry carpet. The bedspread was red silk. An assistant was arranging dozens of pillows in various sizes and shapes on the bed.

"Outfit seven-B?" another assistant asked Joey.

Joey opened her robe. She wore white flannel pajamas with blue clouds on them. The pajama top was cropped so that her belly showed, and the bottoms had a draw string.

This is the first thing I've modeled that I'd actually wear, Joey thought.

"Those aren't seven-B," the assistant said.

Joey looked down at herself. "This is what Laura gave me."

"Hold on," the assistant said. She spoke to someone on her walkie-talkie, then turned back to Joey.

"Someone messed up again. You're supposed to be wearing—"

"Here it iz, I could not wait for ze imbecile who iz supposed to keep zis straight," Véronique said, hurrying over to them with something white and silky in her hand. She handed it to Joey. "Change quickly, *vite, vite*, we are behind!"

Joey looked at the white thing. It was a teddie, a small, transparent silk and lace teddie, with tiny, delicate seed pearls embroidered into the lace.

"Go, go, go!" Véronique ordered.

A screen had been set up in the corner of the room. Joey went behind it and changed into the teddie. It wasn't entirely transparent, but it was sheer enough to show the outline of her body, and the sides were cut so high they ended at her waist.

Oh, God.

"Josephine, let's get a move on," someone begged.

Joey stepped out from behind the screen. Phoebe hurried over to her to touch up her makeup. Dani fussed over her hair. Someone else handed her a diaphanous white lace robe, which went over the teddie. She slipped it on.

Then her eyes slid over to the bed. There sat Aaron Poole, wearing white silk boxer shorts. And nothing else.

"Ready with Josephine?" Alan called.

"Ready," Phoebe said.

Joey walked over to Alan on leaden feet. She didn't look at Aaron, but she could feel his eyes on her.

"What happened to Renaldo?" she asked nonchalantly.

"I changed my mind," Alan explained. "Now, in this shot, A.P. will be carrying you to bed."

Alan reached over and adjusted one of Joey's thin spaghetti straps.

"He's *what?*" Joey squeaked.

"I didn't realize English was a second language for you," Alan said dryly. "This is the honeymoon shot. You two are on your honeymoon. And your new husband is carrying you to bed."

"But . . . but . . . I'm . . . heavy," Joey protested.

Alan looked at her dubiously.

"And I just ate a doughnut! Maybe Sloan could—"

Alan moved close and put his arm around Joey's shoulder. "Josephine, it must be patently clear to you now that you are the only model on this shoot who isn't an experienced professional. I decided to give you a chance because you're the right size and the right shape, and because I had a temporary lapse in sanity. Please don't make me regret it."

Joey gulped hard. "I won't."

"Delightful. Now, go over by the bed, please."

Joey stood by the bed. She stared at the floor. All around her, people were adjusting lights and reflectors.

"Okay, A.P., pick Josephine up, and let's get the light set on you, please," Alan called.

Joey had no choice. She raised her eyes. A.P.— Aaron Poole—was standing right next to her, half naked.

"Hi," he said, looking amused.

"Look, can we just pretend we don't know each other?" Joey said under her breath.

He chuckled. "That's easy, we don't know each other." He held out his arms. "May I?"

Joey nodded mutely.

Aaron easily lifted her into his arms, cradling her against his chest.

"Wait, hold her away from you until we get the light right, your chest makeup will rub off on her!" the stylist screamed.

Aaron obliged. Clearly, it was no effort for him to carry her weight.

"So, come here often?" Aaron asked.

Joey was too embarrassed to think of a witty comeback.

"Okay, ready to shoot," the photographer's assistant called. "You can pull her to you now, A.P."

Someone put music on, only this time it wasn't rock, it was something lush and classical.

The photographer—not Alan, another one—looked into his lens. "Okay, A.P., think honeymoon," he called. "Look down at her like you adore her and you want to make love to her all night long."

Aaron's eyes lowered to Joey. "I adore you, and I want to make love to you all night long," he said.

"Shut up," she replied, gazing up at him.

"Perfect, you two, that's great, awesome, hot," the photographer called as he snapped away. They were slightly repositioned as the shoot went on and on.

"Ready to go to the bed shot," the photographer said, putting his camera down.

"Set up for the bed shot!" an assistant yelled.

"The *what*?" Joey yelped.

Aaron draped one arm around her shoulder. "This is some honeymoon, huh, honey?"

An assistant stripped the robe off Joey. Alan hurried over. "We want you on top of the quilt, Josephine, just there. And A.P., you'll be next to her, braced on one arm, about to kiss her."

Joey felt like barfing. She looked at the bed. She didn't move. She couldn't move.

"Time is money, Josephine," Alan said sharply, hurrying over to the photographer.

"Look, I know this is tough for you," Aaron told her, his voice low. "It's just acting. You're playing a role. So am I. Try pretending you're someone else. Or that I'm someone else, okay?"

Joey nodded. She got onto the bed. Two assistants immediately adjusted her teddie, her hair, then her arms and legs. Then Aaron lay down next to her, and they made the same minute adjustments to him.

"Almost ready," the photographer called.

"Remember, acting," Aaron whispered, his voice kind. "I'm someone else."

"Okay, give me passion, give me heat," the photographer yelled. Someone switched the music, and Ravel's *Bolero* poured out of the sound system.

"Close your eyes, Josephine," the photographer called. "This is your wedding night, you're in ecstasy."

Joey closed her eyes.

He's someone else, Joey thought. He's someone else.

And then, with her eyes tightly closed and the gorgeous music filling the room, he was someone else. Dawson. Dawson was leaning over her, about to kiss her; it was their wedding night.

She didn't even think about what she was doing. Joey lifted her arms, reaching for Dawson. His hands tangled in her hair. His lips were so close to hers now, and . . .

"Great! That was great!" the photographer cried. "Let's move on. Next shot, people."

Joey opened her eyes. Everyone was bustling around, moving lights and equipment, paying no attention at all to her. Or to Aaron. Not Dawson. Aaron.

They both sat up.

"You okay?" he asked her.

Joey nodded.

"Is this your first modeling job?"

She nodded again.

"You did great. Really."

She managed to smile back. "Thanks."

"Yo, A.P., let's move it, we need to change the bed around," an assistant told them.

Aaron helped Joey to her feet. He smiled at her. "Hey, whoever you were thinking of just now . . . he's one lucky guy."

Chapter 12

Joey was in the wardrobe trailer, she'd just been paid, and she gaped at the amount of the huge check in her hands. It was drawn on one of the biggest banks in the area—she'd have no trouble cashing it. Then she could turn over all the money to Bessie.

Of course, she still had to figure out how to explain to Bessie where she'd gotten it.

So much money, just for having her picture taken over and over and pretending she was someone utterly different from who she really was. It didn't seem real or possible. And yet there it was, more money than Bessie's profit at the Ice House for an entire month, even during tourist season.

"And you say looks aren't important, Dawson," Joey mumbled, as if he were really there to hear her. "This is one shallow, superficial, beauty-is-only-skin-deep world."

"Did you say something?" Laura asked her absentmindedly as she checked all the lingerie from the shoot off on her list.

"No," Joey replied. She stashed the check in the back pocket of her jeans and caught a glimpse of herself in the mirror. As soon as the shoot had finished, she'd taken off all the makeup and pulled her hair back with a scrunchie. Faint smudges of eye liner still clung to her eyes, but, other than that, she was back to being her old self.

Which was how she liked it.

"Well, thanks for everything," Joey said. Laura waved but didn't look up from her inventory. Joey picked up her backpack and headed out of the van. It was getting dark, and much colder. She decided to stop at the catering van—it was still functioning for the crew, as they would have to stay on for hours to clean up—and get Pacey something hot to eat. As for the van that would take them back to Boston, it wasn't leaving for another half hour, at least.

Loaded down with fried chicken and all the trimmings, Joey headed for Pacey's spot under the tree.

He wasn't alone.

Sloan Johnson was with him, her makeup gone, dressed in a tiny T-shirt—obviously without a bra—under a brown leather bomber jacket. She also wore baggy jeans that rested low on her hips. They showed off her taut stomach and navel ring.

"Ah, Josephine, future supermodel," Pacey said, grinning.

She thrust the plate at him. "Eat, Buffman."

"Sloan already brought me victuals," Pacey told

her, but he took the plate anyway. He looked at Sloan. "I'm training, you know how it is."

"Oh, wow, I didn't know you trained," Sloan said.

Pacey nodded, his mouth full of fried chicken. "I gave Renaldo a few pointers this afternoon. He asked me."

"Wow," Sloan said, nodding. "I guess I couldn't tell because your clothes are loose." She got up to stretch, which involved her lifting one leg high on the tree, then bringing her head down to her knee, with her arms overhead touching her toe.

Pacey almost choked on a chicken wing as his hormones worked overtime.

"Great flexibility, Sloan. Bet that comes in handy." He gave her what he hoped was a sophisticated, knowing look.

"For what?" she asked, bringing her leg down.

Joey snorted back a laugh. Then she picked up one of the biscuits on Pacey's plate and took a huge bite.

Sloan looked horrified. "There's butter on that!"

"Yeah?" Joey licked some melted butter off her finger.

"Butter has, like, all this fat in it," Sloan explained.

"Huh." Joey reached for the other biscuit.

Sloan watched Joey eat. "Wow. You are so lucky. I gain weight if I even look at food."

"The solution to that is to just stuff it in with your eyes closed," Joey suggested.

Sloan laughed. "You're so funny, Josephine."

"Josephine and I are just friends, did I mention that?" Pacey asked Sloan, out of the blue.

"Once I ate Chinese the night before this bathing-suit catalog job," Sloan confided to them, "and I was so puffy the next day, I had to, like, wrap myself in plastic wrap and shower for thirty minutes."

"Good friends," Pacey added, "but there's just no real spark there between me and Josephine, if you catch my drift. Yeah, I'm one free agent."

Joey looked at Sloan. "Wait. You took a shower covered in *plastic wrap?*"

Sloan nodded. "And even after that, I still had to use Preparation H under my eyes to take down the puffiness."

Joey gagged on the last of the biscuit. Pacey hit her on the back—a little harder than was necessary, she thought.

"Are you okay?" Sloan asked.

"Fine," Joey managed.

Sloan was busy inspecting an inch of skin above her navel ring. "Can you get cellulite on your stomach?"

"I'll check it out for you," Pacey said quickly. He bent over and took a close look at her navel ring.

Sloan giggled. "You're so cute, Pacey." She looked at her watch. "Oh, wow, we'd better get to the van."

"If you're tired, I could carry you," Pacey offered. "I bench-press a whole lot more than you weigh without cracking a sweat."

Sloan giggled. "Well, I am kind of tired."

"Gee, I'd love to stay and watch this touching

Neanderthal mating ritual, but I'm all watched out," Joey said. "See you in the van." She went on ahead.

"Who's Neanderthal?" Sloan asked Pacey.

In answer, he swept her up in his arms. And almost keeled over.

"Oh, wow," she giggled. "You're so strong!"

"No problem," Pacey said through gritted teeth. "Uh, how far away is the van?"

"Over there," Sloan pointed. Pacey began to carry her toward the van, making a desperate effort not to wheeze audibly.

"Gee, Pacey, you're a sweetheart. If you weren't Josephine's boyfriend, I would definitely ask you out."

"Remember how I told you she isn't really my girlfriend?" Pacey said between grunts.

"Oh, wow, really? Did you say that?" Sloan exclaimed.

Pacey set her down, breathing hard. "I like to look a woman as beautiful as you are in the eye."

"That's so sweet," Sloan cooed. "But wait, are you sure you and Josephine aren't, you know?"

"We're so not 'you know,' you can't even imagine," Pacey said. "I'm more her . . . big brother. I try to watch out for her, you know, help mold the ol' career."

"I wish I had someone to do that for me," Sloan said.

"Say no more," Pacey replied. "I'm your man."

Sloan hugged him. "You are just too sweet, Pacey Buffman." The two of them scrambled into the van. Sloan slid into the seat in front of Joey and pulled Pacey in next to her. She twisted around in her seat.

"Listen, Josephine, I just want to be extra-special certain that you and Pacey aren't together. He's really, really cute, but I never poach another model's guy."

"Poach away," Joey assured her.

"Josephine's boyfriend is actually my best friend," Pacey explained. "His name is Dawson."

"So, do you guys all go to college with Pacey?" Sloan asked Joey.

"College?" Joey repeated.

"Hey, let's not talk about school," Pacey said quickly.

"I just got the greatest idea!" Sloan exclaimed. "Tomorrow night, the four of us should double-date. Pacey and me and you and this guy Dawson. That'd be so awesome!"

"Gee, I don't think—" Joey began.

"Great idea!" Pacey boomed.

"Pacey," Joey said, "would you come up to the front of the van with me? There's a cooler of bottled water out there, and Sloan wants some."

Sloan held up a bottle of water. "Got some already!"

"That one has calories," Joey told her.

"Oh, wow, are you sure?" Sloan read the label on the bottle.

Joey dragged Pacey out of the van. "Are you out of your mind?" she hissed.

"Did you see that girl, Jocy? She's a walking centerfold, and she just asked me out."

"Pacey, Sloan makes driftwood look intelligent. If she says 'Oh, wow' one more time, I will be forced to put her out of my misery."

"Maybe she's just shy," Pacey suggested.

"Yuh. And maybe her name isn't Sloan, it's Slow Ann."

Pacey grabbed Joey and flung her backward into a romantic dip. "Oh, Josephine, you're beautiful when you're jealous."

"Do you want to live?" Joey asked him.

He righted her and stepped aside as Renaldo and Royce got on the van. "Okay, so maybe she's never going to work for NASA," Pacey told her. "But no girl who looks like that ever asked me out before. Come to think of it, no *girl* ever asked me out before—but that's beside the point. I really want to say yes."

"So say yes. Just leave me out of it."

"I can't." Pacey hesitated. "It's just possible that the Buff Man is not entirely confident about going out with her alone."

"What, a stud muffin like you?" Joey asked.

"She asked us to double. So I'm asking you for a favor, Joey." There was no pretense in Pacey's voice now. "It's just one night. You and Dawson, me and Sloan. It would mean a lot to me."

"What about Andie?" Joey asked, folding her arms.

"It was Andie's idea for us to see other people," Pacey reminded her. "I never thought I'd really have anyone else to see."

"But—"

"I was there for you, Joey," Pacey said. "You asked for a big favor, I said yes. Well, now I'm asking."

Sloan knocked on the van window and waved at him. He waved back. She blew Pacey a kiss.

"I'm gonna throw up," Joey said. Pacey gave her puppy-dog eyes and nuzzled against her like a young cocker spaniel.

She pushed him away. "If you promise to stop that, the answer is, I'll do it."

"Yes!" Pacey pumped one fist in the air. He kissed her cheek. "Love ya, babe." He climbed back onto the van and sat with Sloan.

Joey got on slowly. She noticed Aaron was sitting by himself, near the front. "How's it going?" he asked her. "Wanna sit?"

She sat next to him. Meanwhile, Véronique finished counting heads and told the driver to go, go, go.

"Have fun today?" Aaron asked her.

"I made money," Joey said, pushing some stray hair off her face.

"Yeah, this catalog pays great," he agreed. "A lot more than figure modeling for art class. But these gigs are hard to come by."

She nodded and stared straight ahead. "Listen, Aaron, I need for you to do me a favor."

"Sure, what?"

"Don't tell anyone back at school about this."

His eyebrows shot up. "Big secret, huh?"

"I can't explain," Joey said, still not looking at him. "So, will you do it?"

He studied her tense profile in the fading light. "Hey," he finally said, "it never happened. What modeling shoot?"

Chapter 13

Joey, Dawson, Pacey, and Sloan stood in the long movie line. Dawson was telling Sloan all about his latest student film; she kept nodding her head and saying "Wow." Pacey, meanwhile, looked like the cat who had eaten the proverbial canary.

Joey rolled her eyes and sighed. She had been so certain that Dawson would never go for Pacey's lame cover story: he'd met Sloan when she was walking her dog down by the docks, the two of them had gotten to talking, and Sloan had mentioned her interest in independent films. So Pacey had thought, why not do a double-date with my friend the independent filmmaker and my other friend Joey, who not only was a sometimes model but was—ta-da!—an independent film actress.

Yuh.

I will never again underestimate Dawson's desire

to be called an independent filmmaker, Joey thought as the line for the new Stanley Kubrick film moved forward.

". . . so essentially what I'm trying to say in my movie is that surface beauty is basically meaningless," Dawson concluded.

"Oh, wow," Slow Ann breathed, nodding seriously. "I get it."

"Well, you're astute about these things," Pacey told her, proprietorially dropping his arm around her shoulders.

Joey rolled her eyes. Slow Ann was wearing a long stretchy skirt with a slit all the way up one thigh and a tiny, sheer black lace shirt over a black lace bra. Pacey kept looking around. It was pathetically obvious to Joey that he was hoping to see people he knew, who would notice that Pacey Witter was out with a major babe.

"You okay, Joey?" Dawson asked her.

"Sure. Why wouldn't I be okay?" Joey thrust her hands into the pockets of her baggy cargo pants. Pacey was whispering in Slow Ann's ear, and she giggled in response. "I mean, so what if he's marginally more pathetic than, say, the loser guy in *Something About Mary*."

"I'm happy to see him happy." Dawson shrugged. "And remember that it's Andie who—"

"Wanted space," Joey finished. "I know, I know. But at least Andie has a functional IQ. Slow Ann over there was clearly in the 'Oh, wow' line when brains got handed out."

"Maybe she's shy. Everyone doesn't share your

facility with words, Joey. Give her a chance—she's very interested in film."

She gave Dawson a level look. "It's like I'm seeing you in an entirely new light."

Dawson looked bewildered. "What?"

Just then, a collective groan went up from the twenty or so people left in line. A small SOLD OUT sign had been taped up in the ticket booth. Then another sign went up under it: TICKETS BEING SOLD FOR 10 P.M. ONLY.

"Let's stay," Dawson suggested. "We can buy tickets, then go someplace and talk."

"I'd love to hear about what it's like for you guys in college," Slow Ann said. "Did you ever see one of those issues of *Playboy* devoted to college girls?"

Dawson looked confused.

"Bowling!" Pacey blurted out, turning to Sloan. He put on a fake French accent and imitated Véronique. "We can go, go, go! Eet is very retro-chic, no?"

"Sorry, I don't speak French," Slow Ann said.

Joey shot Dawson a meaningful look.

Bowl-a-Rama was not far from where they were. The place was hopping, but they were able to rent shoes, get scorecards and tiny pencils, and be assigned a lane.

"Oh, wow, this is so fun!" Sloan exclaimed. "Isn't it fun, Josephine?"

"Words fail me," Joey replied, changing shoes.

"Hey, Josephine, wouldn't this be a great place for a modeling shoot?"

"You model?" Dawson asked Sloan.

"Of course! Wow, didn't Pacey tell you anything?"

"Okay, who's going first?" Pacey asked, too heartily. "Looks like it's you, Sloan."

"You can go, Pacey." She sat next to Dawson. "I'm so, like, lucky, because ever since I was a little girl, I wanted to be a model, and now I really am one."

"Bummer, two gutter balls," Pacey said, hurrying back to them. "Your turn, Sloan!"

"Josephine can go," Sloan offered.

"Fine." Joey grabbed a ball and moved into the lane.

Sloan leaned toward Dawson. "At first I thought I'd never make it, because my breasts are too big. In comparison to, like, my waist and hips, you know?"

"Uh . . ." was all Dawson could muster.

"But then I got this bikini calendar gig, and then I found out that if you have my kind of measurements, you can get all this bathing suit and lingerie work, like for hot-rod magazines. Lucky me, huh?"

Dawson gave Sloan a jaded look. "And I suppose you want to go from modeling to acting in films, right?"

"Oh, wow, that would be super!" Sloan cried. "Lauren Hutton is, like, my god."

Dawson folded his arms. "Kubrick is a genius, don't you think? He shows such incredible range between *2001* and *A Clockwork Orange*. But then there's what he did with *Barry Lyndon*. What do you think, Sloan?"

She shrugged. "Sorry, I don't know Barry."

Pacey yanked her up. "Time to bowl, Sloan. Show us the way."

"Oh, wait, I know Halle Berry!" Sloan said as Pacey pointed her toward the lane. "She started out as a model, too, you know. And Cameron Diaz. And Kathy Ireland, except her voice is kind of squeaky like Minnie Mouse—"

"Here's your ball, Sloan," Pacey said. "Bowl."

"Oh, wow, okay." She stepped to the top of the lane, eyed the pins, and went for it.

Pacey played close attention to the rear view. "Poetry in motion," he sighed.

Joey slumped down next to Dawson. "Are we having fun yet?"

"Pacey, you told me she was interested in *independent* films," Dawson said.

"Did I say that?"

"Oh, wow, did you guys see that? I almost got a strike!" Sloan cried as nine pins crashed and fell.

"Great!" Pacey called.

Dawson shook his head. "Those herbal supplements are getting to your brain, assuming, of course, that you actually have one. What are you doing with her?"

"Oh, wow, gutter ball," Sloan groaned as she rolled again. "I was really close, though."

"Could it be you're just a tad jealous that I'm out with such a babe?" Pacey asked Dawson.

"Jealous?" Dawson said incredulously.

Sloan trotted over to them. "Hey, Josephine, wanna come to the john with me?"

"No, thanks."

"Okay, well, be right back," Sloan promised.

"That's what I'm afraid of," Joey mumbled.

Dawson made sure Sloan was out of hearing distance. "Okay, Pacey, what's really going on here?"

"We're on this double date—"

"The only relationship Sloan has with film is when her sunglasses fog up," Dawson said. "How can you go from a girl like Andie to a girl like this?"

"I realize that reality is not necessarily a concept with which you have more than a passing acquaintance," Pacey told Dawson, "so as your friend, allow me to spell it out for you. Kingdoms have fallen for girls who look like Sloan. Girls who look like Sloan rule the world. Every guy wants one. Unlike you, I am honest enough to admit it."

"It's not what I want," Dawson insisted. "I mean, for example, look at Joey."

Joey jumped up, her eyes blazing. "Thank you, Dawson, for using me to prove your point. I realize I should be pathetically grateful that you ever gave a bowser such as myself the time of day—"

"You know that isn't what I meant, Joey, come on." Dawson stood up, too. "I was talking about what's really important."

"Enlighten me," Joey said.

"Who you really are. The essential Joey, not the package that houses her," Dawson said softly.

"That is beautiful," Pacey said, choking up and holding his throat dramatically. "Of course, if Joey looked like Emily LaPaz, it would have to be a really big house."

"You're a deeper person than this, Pacey," Dawson told him. "You don't have to stoop to this kind of—"

"Pacey Buffman!" Sloan squealed as she took a running leap and threw herself into Pacey's arms. "You are just too cute to live!" She kissed him on the cheek.

Pacey wrapped his arms around Sloan's slender waist. "I'll give you six hours to stop that shocking behavior," he told her.

She giggled and kissed him again. This time, Pacey kissed her back. On the lips.

"Hi, Pacey," said a female voice.

Pacey looked up, his arms still around Sloan.

He was looking directly at Andie.

He dropped his arms as if Sloan were on fire. "Andie! Hi!"

She glared at him. Then she turned around and walked away.

"Uh, will you excuse me?" Pacey told Sloan. "I need to go . . . talk to my friend."

"Sure," Sloan said blithely. "Hey, bring her over to meet us."

Pacey ran to catch Andie, just before she got out the door. "Andie, wait."

"Wait for what?"

"Well, didn't you come in to bowl?" Pacey asked.

"Gee, my bowling get-up-and-go seems to have got up and went. Jack can bowl by himself. I'm outta here."

"Wait! Look, Andie, this isn't what it looks like."

Andie put her hands on her hips. "What does it look like, Pacey? Who's that girl?"

"That girl? Over there?" Pacey's mind went completely blank. "That's . . . Special Agent Starling."

"Special Agent Starling. Nice try, Pacey. Jodie

Foster. *Silence of the Lambs*. And right now I'm about as attracted to you as I was to the guy in the cell next to Hannibal Lecter's."

"Okay, that was dumb," Pacey admitted.

"Good, now we're getting somewhere," Andie replied. "Try the truth."

Pacey nodded. "The truth. The truth is, she's . . . Joey's cousin. From Florida."

"You are such a liar—"

"Okay, you're right." Pacey turned his hands up. "I'm on a date, okay? Her name is Sloan. Now, you tell me why I feel so guilty when you're the one who told me—in fact, practically ordered me—to go out with other people."

Silence. Then, finally, "I suppose it's one thing to decide we should see other people in theory," Andie said slowly, "and another to have it shoved in your face."

"I didn't shove this in your face. You walked in here."

Andie looked past Pacey and checked Sloan out again. "So where did you meet her? Don't tell me, she's a model with the IQ of an eggplant."

"Hey, give me a little more credit, okay?" Pacey asked, using his best wounded voice. "It so happens she's premed. At . . . Boston College."

"Hey, Pacey," Jack said, walking over to them. "You bowling, Andie, or not?"

"Not," Andie said. "I suddenly have this really bad headache. You go ahead." She waited for her brother to walk away, then took Pacey's hand. "Listen, I just want to say . . . I wasn't fair before. You're right."

"That can't be," Pacey said. "I'm never right."

"I'm serious," Andie insisted. "You can see whoever you want. I don't have any right to get all bent out of shape over it."

"Yes, you do—"

"In fact, I'm perfectly fine with it," Andie went on. "It was just the shock. Okay. So. We're cool. We're groovy. Ob-la-di, ob-la-da, life goes on, right?"

"Andie—"

"Catch you later, Pacey," Andie said. "Have fun." She disappeared out into the night.

Sloan ran over to Pacey and wrapped her arms around his neck. "Oh, wow, where did your friend go?"

"I don't know," Pacey said. "Let's go bowl."

Suddenly, Sloan's arms didn't feel quite as fantastic as they had before.

Chapter 14

Joey paced nervously across her bedroom, back and forth, back and forth, as she waited for the doorbell to ring.

During her lunch break at school that day, she'd gone to the Capeside branch of the bank on which her check from La Petite Liz Bette had been drawn and presented it at a teller window to be cashed in full.

Her stomach had been tied up in knots while she waited—some bank officer had to be called to authorize payment on the check. He had eyebrows so bushy they looked like two fat black caterpillars taking a little snooze over his eyes. When he saw the size of Joey's check, the caterpillars jumped on his forehead, and he asked Joey for three forms of ID. Fortunately, she'd come prepared.

Then he'd asked, "Are you sure you wouldn't

rather open an account? As a young person, this could be the beginning of a frugal savings plan."

Savings plan. High amusement factor there.

"Just cash the check, please," Joey had instructed. "In hundred-dollar bills."

That had caused the caterpillars to jump again, but finally he'd authorized the transaction, and Joey had walked out of the bank with an envelope under her arm that was stuffed with hundred-dollar bills.

She'd carried that envelope around at school all day, not taking the chance of putting it in her locker. Every two seconds, she touched it, to make sure that it was still there.

That envelope was her and Bessie's ticket out of disaster.

After school, she'd asked Pacey one more favor. Could he please, between six and seven this evening, leave the envelope on the doorstep, ring the bell to their house, then run away? And run fast?

Pacey was happy to say yes. He knew exactly what was in the envelope, and he was also in a particularly good mood. It seemed that both Andie and Slow Ann had called him—Andie to say that she was rethinking what she had said about needing more space, Slow Ann to see if he wanted to go out again.

"And Pacey, if Bessie ever asks you, you have no idea where that money came from," Joey had added.

Now Joey looked at her watch again. It was six-fifty, where was Pacey? Bessie was in the kitchen baking cookies, while Alexander was in his playpen. Bessie had decided to try to get a baking business off the ground as a way of earning some extra money. So far, she had exactly one customer, for whom she was currently baking organic oatmeal raisin cookies.

Still pacing, Joey checked her watch again. Six fifty-three. What if someone had robbed Pacey on his way here? What if he lost the money? What if Deputy Doug found the envelope in Pacey's room? He'd put Pacey in jail, because he'd think he was dealing drugs and—

Ding-dong!

Joey rushed to her window and looked out. Pacey was running as fast as he could away from the house. Then he dodged to the left, rounded a corner, and was out of sight.

Joey's hands grew clammy. Bessie had to be at the door now, picking up the envelope. Opening the envelope. Looking inside. She's stunned—there's so much money! She can't believe it. She looks around—no one is there. She looks at the money again, and then she sees there's a note. She reads the note. She yells for me—

"Joey!" Bessie screamed. "Oh, my God, Joey!"

"Okay, Josephine," Joey muttered. "This is your chance to give an Academy Award–level performance."

"What?" Joey asked as she entered the front room. "Are you okay?"

Bessie stood in the living room, a sea of hundred-dollar bills scattered on the tattered carpeting. Tears were running down her cheeks.

"Is it Monopoly money?" Joey asked.

Bessie shook her head. "It's real," she whispered.

Joey kneeled to pick up a hundred-dollar bill. "Where did you get it?"

"I don't know," Bessie said, and she began laughing through her tears. "An angel!"

Joey looked at her skeptically. "A what?"

"Someone rang the doorbell, and when I opened the door, no one was there, just this envelope full of money. And this note." She handed it to Joey.

Yuh, like I don't know what this says—I wrote it—Joey thought. So it really surprised her when reading her own words brought tears to her eyes.

"To Bessie," it read, "for the Ice House, from someone in Capeside who loves you very, very much."

"Incredible," Joey said, handing the note back to Bessie.

"Joey, if I'm dreaming right now, don't ever wake me up." Bessie hesitated, then pinched her own arm, hard. "That hurt. I'm not dreaming. But things like this don't happen in real life!"

"How much is it?" Joey asked.

"I counted it," Bessie said, "and with the money from the catering gig, we're only five hundred dollars short to call in the plumbers, providing we live on noodles and powdered cheese for a couple of weeks."

Bessie sat heavily on the couch. "So many bad things have happened to us, Joey. I mean, you just get used to it after a while. You just make up your mind that that's how the world is, you know?"

Joey knelt in front of her. "But it isn't," she said softly. "Not always."

She bit her lower lip pensively. So often Bessie

drove her nuts, acting as if she was Joey's mother, expecting Joey to drop everything to take care of Alexander. But Bessie hadn't asked for all the bad stuff that had happened to her any more than Joey had. And when you got right down to it, all they had was each other. And that was more important than her stupid pride.

"Bessie?"

"What?"

"I have five hundred dollars."

"Wait, did you just say—"

Joey nodded. "It'll take an hour or so to get it."

She went to the telephone in the kitchen and punched in Dawson's familiar number.

"Hello?"

"It's me," Joey said. "Look, I'm gonna cut right to the chase here, Dawson, because this isn't the easiest phone call in the world for me to make. You know that Sandy Koufax baseball card you sold? And the earrings Jen's mom bought her as a bribe? Well, Bessie and I would very much like to borrow what you offered, Dawson. A simple yes or no will do."

From the other end of the phone, silence.

"Dawson?"

"Joey," he said in his special Dawson way. And then he added: "Yes."

Chapter 15

Dawson looked over at Joey, who was taping old-fashioned cutouts of girls in poodle skirts and guys in saddle shoes to the walls of the Ice House. He couldn't help smiling. She looked so happy, and it seemed to Dawson that she hadn't looked happy in a long time. Her face just lit up—there, just like that—and her beauty came from someplace so much deeper than her skin.

Dawson thought back on how much had happened in such a short period of time, since Bessie and Joey had somehow gotten all the money they needed to fix the Ice House. Contractors had taken over, and the floor of the Ice House had been torn up. The old pipes were taken out, new pipes were relaid, the sewage system was tested and retested, and the state health inspector gave his blessing.

And now Dawson, Jen, and Joey were at the Ice

House, putting the finishing touches on the place for the big reopening. A new sign had replaced the old, sad one saying that the place was closed. This sign read:

ICE HOUSE GRAND REOPENING PARTY: SATURDAY NIGHT. COME DRESSED IN YOUR FIFTIES BEST, FIFTIES PRICES!

Bessie had decided that in honor of their anonymous angel, she'd roll the prices in the Ice House back to what they were when the place opened in 1955. Hot dogs would be a quarter, ice cream sodas fifty cents, and a cheeseburger deluxe, served on a hard roll with lettuce and tomato and a side of fries, was sixty-nine cents.

Dawson and Jen had volunteered to help deal with the opening-night crowd. Like Joey, they were both dressed in fifties outfits cobbled together from a thrift shop and a trunk in Grams's attic. Dawson had on baggy flannel pants, while Jen wore a straight black skirt that came to her calves and a tight red sweater over a bullet bra.

Joey, who now stood on a chair, dangling paper jitterbugging couples from the ceiling, had found a felt circle skirt on which she'd drawn a poodle with magic marker, and her hair was up in a high ponytail. Dawson smiled. Joey looked so intent as she worked, her long ponytail fell carelessly down her back—

"You're staring, Dawson," Jen said bluntly, coming up next to him.

"I was . . . framing my shot," Dawson explained. He picked up his video camera and aimed it at Joey.

"For my documentary. 'The Ice House: Rebuilding a Dream.'"

Jen leaned against a table. "I have to say, I feel good about this. That in some minute way I helped make it happen, I mean."

"Me, too." Dawson's camera followed Joey as she went over to the jukebox and pressed on some music. Elvis singing "Blue Suede Shoes" filled the air.

"Hey, when are we opening, Bessie?" Jack called from the front of the restaurant. "The natives are restless."

Though it was early, a crowd had already gathered outside, many of them dressed in their fifties best. The whole town was anxious to celebrate the re-opening of the Ice House, especially at fifties prices.

"Lemme just come out there and check everything one last time!" Bessie called back.

"Decorating is evidently not my forte," Joey said, parking her butt on the table where Dawson and Jen sat. "My little paper fifties characters look major cheesy."

"The fifties was a cheesy decade," Dawson said, following Bessie with his camera as she hustled out of the kitchen. She wore rolled-up jeans, an oversized man's shirt, and saddle shoes.

"It looks great in here," Bessie pronounced, throwing her arms wide. "I love this place, and I'll never take it for granted again. It's home."

"There's no place like home, there's no place like home," Joey chanted, doing her best Dorothy imitation from *The Wizard of Oz.*

"Forget Dorothy," Jen said. "I just realized something. You're Sandy Dumbrowski, and I'm Rizzo."

Joey shrugged. "Grease is definitely the word back in that kitchen tonight. Greasy burgers, greasy fries, greasy—"

"I meant in life," Jen interrupted. "I'm the bad girl with the tough exterior and the vulnerable heart. You're the good girl—"

"Who tramps herself up to get a mental midget like Danny Zuko?" Joey asked archly. "I don't think so." She jumped off the table and went over to her sister. "Is it show time?"

Bessie looked at the growing crowd outside, then she hugged Joey. "I wish Mom was here to see this."

A lump rose in Joey's throat, but she willed it down. "She'd be really proud of you, Bessie." She hugged her sister back.

"Alrighty, then," Bessie said. "Let's do it. Jack, unlock the door. Let the games begin!"

Two hours later, the Ice House was so packed it was difficult to move. Old rock music blared from the jukebox. Some people were attempting to dance between the tables. Joey, Jen, Dawson, and two community college girls hired for the evening rushed around, taking and delivering orders, while Bessie and Jack flipped burgers and deep-fried french fries in the kitchen.

"Hey, Joey, great party!" a girl from Joey's English class said as she dodged by with her boyfriend.

"Thanks," Joey said on the run. It was impossible to keep up with the orders, they were coming so fast. She slapped three order slips on the wheel and pushed her unkempt hair off her face.

"Orders up," Jack yelled as he shoved plates of burgers and fries under the heat lamp.

Jen added two more orders to the wheel. "This is a zoo, huh?"

Joey puffed air up through her lower lip. "Andie's out of town for the weekend, but I should have asked Pacey to help tonight. I just didn't know it would be this crazy."

"Oh, I asked Pacey for you, actually," Jen said. "He said he had a big date."

"Oh, great," Joey groaned. "It has to be Slow Ann."

"Who?" Jen asked.

"Order up!" Jack barked. "Come on, you guys, pick up the food!"

Joey and Jen picked up the plates and hurried into the crowd. Jen set hers in front of a packed table of college guys near the front door, just as Pacey sauntered in, a gorgeous tall blond in a skin-tight skirt on his arm.

"Who's *that*?" Jen asked.

Pacey sauntered over to her and kissed her cheek. "Jen, how goes it?"

"How does it look like it goes?" Jen asked over the roar of the crowd.

"Oh, wow, major party, huh?" the girl commented.

"Sloan, this is Jen," Pacey said. "Jen, Sloan. Sloan's a model," he added, his arm around her waist.

"I see Dawson!" Sloan cried, standing on her tiptoes. "He's got his video camera. Hey, I wanna be in his movie!"

"Stick with me, and—" Pacey began, but Sloan was already pushing her way through the crowd toward Dawson.

"Lovely girl," Jen commented sarcastically. "Your soul-mate?"

"Yo, waitress," a guy yelled in Jen's direction. "Can we see a little service?"

"Hey, I ordered hot dogs, not burgers," another guy called.

"Jen! Hey, Jen!" from a table of six girls.

Pacey grabbed Jen's order pad. "I'll take that table of girls and the middle-aged bobby-soxers behind them," Pacey said. "You take the other two tables."

"I thought you couldn't help out because of your date," Jen reminded him.

"She appears to be temporarily occupied with her burgeoning film career," Pacey replied.

Many hours later, the crowd had thinned out considerably. A few couples were slow dancing to Bobby Vinton, the college girls were bussing the dirty tables, and Jen, Pacey, and Sloan sat at a table, eating burgers and fries. Actually, Pacey and Jen ate, and Sloan watched. Joey sat at the counter, dazed from exhaustion. Dawson was still filming. His camera panned the front door, just as it opened.

And in walked Katrina Turner, the gorgeous girl Dawson had walked in on at school, the classical cellist.

Dawson felt a little jump of excitement. He kept the camera on her as she walked gracefully over to an empty table and sat down.

Still filming, Dawson walked over to her. "You missed the party," he said.

"I didn't know there was one until I read the sign outside just now," she replied. "What's the camera for?"

"My documentary film on the Ice House."

"Well, I'm not very photogenic," she demurred. "You might want to leave me out."

"I'm seeing you from behind the lens right now," Dawson said, "and I would have to say that you are extremely photogenic. It's a question of light. The reflection of light, really."

"And I reflect light?"

"You're luminous. From a video perspective, I mean."

She smiled. "Thanks. Is there a waitress, or—"

"Right here."

Dawson turned around. Joey was standing behind him.

"May I take your luminous order?" Joey asked, her tone poisonous.

Katrina ordered, and Joey stomped off.

"Oh, wow," Sloan squealed as the music changed. " 'Rock around the Clock,' I love this song." She jumped up to dance. "Hey, Dawson, you should get this on film!"

"Dawson, is that your first name or your last name?" Katrina asked.

"First. It's Dawson Leery." He looked over his shoulder at Joey, who stood behind the counter, her back to him.

"Nice to meet you, Dawson Leery," Katrina said. "I'm—"

"I know who you are."

"You do?"

"Actually, I heard you play once. In the music room at school. I just happened to be walking by. You were playing something by Casals, right?"

She smiled. "I'm impressed. Sit with me," she offered.

He lifted the camera again. "I'd rather film you." Looking at her through the lens, he felt so much less self-conscious. The camera slid over her long, gleaming hair, her perfect features, the graceful curve of her neck, leading to—

"Burger and fries," Joey said, slamming a plate down in front of Katrina. "Would you like to choke down a Coke with that?"

"No, thanks," Katrina said.

Joey ignored Dawson and went to join Jen and Pacey. Sloan danced on by herself.

The door opened again, and a guy Dawson recognized from the school football team came in. He spotted Katrina and went right over to her, kissing her lightly on the lips before he sat down. "Sorry I'm late," he told her, then he eyed Dawson.

"I'm making a documentary," Dawson explained quickly. Still filming, he backed away from the table and went to sit with Pacey, Jen, and Joey. Joey pointedly ignored him.

"Rock, around, the clock tonight!" Sloan sang at the top of her lungs as she danced, clearly hoping to get Dawson's attention.

"Isn't it past her bedtime or something?" Jen asked Pacey.

"If she shared her bedtime with me, Jen, neither

of us would be here right now." Pacey pulled out one of his little cellophane packets of vitamins and tore it open, popping the pills into his mouth.

"You're still taking that stuff?" Dawson asked.

Pacey nodded, downing the pills with a glass of water. He watched Sloan dance. "Now, that's what I call talent."

"This obsession with the physical is truly beneath you," Dawson chided him.

"You're above such things, right, Dawson?" Joey sneered.

"I'm just pointing out that since Pacey's interest in Sloan is based solely on the physical, it feeds into his insecurities about his own body, perpetuating this mindless cycle in search of some kind of physical perfection—"

"Not this again," Jen groaned. "Dawson, there's only one man on the planet who doesn't care about looks—some monk in Tibet who lives on a mountain contemplating his navel because there aren't any female monks around."

"But if there were," Joey added pointedly, "I'm sure the monk would notice how the female monks' luminous skin reflected the light."

Dawson shook his head. "You completely misunderstood that conversation, Joey."

"I completely have no interest in that conversation, Dawson."

"Hey, isn't anyone going to dance with me?" Sloan called.

"That's my cue," Pacey said, getting up and dancing over to Sloan.

"What is up with her?" Jen asked. "She's so

dense she doesn't even realize that Pacey is lying to her about his age. He told her he's eighteen, and she believed him."

"It must be his newly ripped biceps," Joey said.

Jen shrugged. "He looks the same to me."

"Hey, Joey, I could use some help," Bessie called from behind the counter, where she was refilling salt and pepper shakers.

"Duty calls." Joey pushed out of her chair.

Impetuously, Dawson went after her. "Are you okay?"

"I'm great. The Ice House is open again, everything's fine, Dawson."

"Oh. Good."

The music changed to something slow, and Pacey took Sloan into his arms. Dawson remembered exactly how it felt to have Joey in his arms like that, how even though she had claimed to hate slow dancing, they had fit together so perfectly, two halves of a whole.

Except that the other half dropped you, he reminded himself. So why was the other half so ticked about his conversation with Katrina, then?

He looked at Joey. She looked back. She was standing so close. He could see into her soul.

He reached out and touched her hair. "Joey, I—"

"Hey, Joey, I mean it," Bessie called. "Move it."

And then she was gone.

Chapter 16

Joey was lost in thought Monday morning as she trudged into school through the side door near the gym. Saturday night had been a smash success, and the Sunday brunch crowd had been so huge, customers had to wait for a table. Usually that only happened during peak tourist season.

This was wonderful, of course. But ever since the night before, Bessie had been obsessing aloud about who her angel might be. This morning she'd actually made a list of possible people while she was drinking her coffee, and she had only stopped because she had to get Alexander changed.

At least I wasn't on her little angel list, Joey thought. But I really just wish she'd drop the whole thing.

Joey headed along the corridor to her nearby locker. As usual, the football players were hanging out by the gym before first period. Brain-dead, Joey thought. Big bodies, little minds. But on Monday mornings, they were usually too busy lying about how far they'd gotten with their girlfriends, or how wrecked they'd gotten at a party over the weekend, to pay any attention to her.

But this time, as soon as they saw Joey, they started whispering and laughing, nudging and high-fiving each other.

"Hey, Potter!" Mark Garrett yelled. "Why do you hide that hot bod of yours under baggy clothes?"

"Ya gotta pay her before she strips," his buddy, Neil Grecco, crowed. He pulled a five-dollar bill out of his wallet and waved it in the air. "This do it, babe?"

Testosterone on parade, Joey thought as she kept walking. Baggy clothes made her at least somewhat invisible to the jocks, which was exactly the way she wanted it.

Joey had almost made it to the locker when Mark broke rank and came over to her. His huge wide-end body blocked her way.

"Move," Joey said.

"Joey, Joey, Joey." Mark leaned one beefy arm on the wall as his friends egged him on. "You know, I hardly recognized you with your clothes on."

"What's the problem, Garrett, didn't get any this weekend? Feeling a little peevish, are we?" Joey asked.

Mark's friends hooted with glee. Joey tried to feint around Mark, but he blocked her. "So, what's Aaron Poole like in the sack, Potter? He man enough for you, baby?"

This time Joey managed to dodge under his arm. She hurried to her locker. Last week, the Capeside High spin machine had churned out the lie that the model from Advanced Life Drawing was hot and heavy with Jen. Evidently, this week it was Joey's turn.

"Ooh, Aaron, you're such a stud!" a guy called to Joey in a high falsetto voice as she spun her locker open.

"Take me, you brute!" his friend added, his voice even higher. They made kissing noises at Joey as they ran down the hall.

It went on all day. Joey was just glad that Dawson was out with a cold, because she really did not want to endure the rumor mill and Dawson's reaction to it at the same time.

By the time she got into Advanced Life Drawing, she was fuming. She made sure to get there early, so she could confront Aaron without anyone over-hearing them.

He was already in place, wearing his bathrobe, reading a paperback copy of *A Midsummer Night's Dream*.

Joey marched over to him. "Did you start it?"

He looked up from his book. "Hello to you, too."

"All day long, the lower life forms of this prison quaintly known as high school have been hooting over our big love affair. Since it does not exist, I would like to know if you started the rumor that it did."

"Why would I do that?"

"I really hate people who answer a question with a question," Joey snapped.

Aaron smiled. "Word gets around fast."

"That is so not funny."

Aaron lifted his book. " 'What fools these mortals be,' huh? No, Joey, I did not start a rumor that we are lovers. However, I do admit that some stray salacious thoughts about you may have crossed my mind at the photo shoot."

Joey could feel herself blushing, but she stood her ground. "Well, just . . . uncross your mind, then."

Aaron shrugged. "You're a beautiful girl."

"I am not even in the ballpark of beautiful."

Aaron shook his head. "You know what I really hate? Beautiful girls who insist that they aren't beautiful."

"I'm not . . . it isn't me."

"Look, you just made a lot of money because of your looks, Joey. No one at that shoot cared about your brains, or your character, or how much Shakespeare you've read. What they cared about is whether your face and body can sell a fantasy to women who weren't blessed with your face and body, so that those women will buy a certain company's underwear. And they'll buy that certain company's underwear because they want to look like you. So do me a favor, and try to be just the tiniest bit grateful for gifts you did nothing to deserve, okay?"

"I'm sorry. If I had known you were going to deliver a sanctimonious lecture, I would have taken notes." Joey whirled around and headed for her seat, just as kids began to stream into the room. Just who the hell did Aaron think he was, anyway? He didn't know her, or anything about her. He probably really did start those rumors about me, Joey thought, angrily pulling her sketch pad out of her backpack.

"So, is it true about you and Aaron?" Nicole Graff called over to Joey.

"No," Joey said through clenched teeth.

Andie hurried in and slid into her seat. "Give me every detail about you and Aaron," Andie told Joey. "I am desperate for a few vicarious thrills in my pathetic excuse for a life."

"There are no details, because there is no me and Aaron," Joey snapped.

"Really?" Andie sounded disappointed.

"Really," Joey echoed. "But cheer up, because tomorrow the rumor mill will have him with you."

Andie considered that for a moment. "That might work wonders in the make-Pacey-jealous department."

"Andie, I hope you don't mind if I'm blunt here, but I'm just a little too stressed at the moment to beat around the bush," Joey said as she took out her charcoal. "Why did you break up with Pacey if you want to make Pacey jealous? Adolescent game-playing is a major waste of time. It sucks just about as much as the adolescent rumor mill."

Andie fiddled with a button on her sweater. "I know you're right. But didn't you ever . . . didn't you ever just feel like everything in your life was too much pressure?"

"Who, me?" Joey asked sarcastically.

"Okay, stupid question," Andie acknowledged.

"Pacey loves you, Andie. And you love him. He's so amazingly improved since you came into his life that it's scary."

Andie nodded. "Right. And it scared him. But no one thought about how it might just scare me, too."

"I guess that's true," Joey acknowledged.

"Is it true that Pacey took that bimbo to the Ice House party Saturday night. Or is that rumor a lie, too?"

"You were out of town."

"So?"

"Why do I feel like a broken record here? It wasn't his idea to see other people."

Andie tapped her pencil against her hand. "Well, maybe I was wrong."

"So tell Pacey, don't tell me."

"He's looking at you," Andie said.

"Pacey? He isn't even in—"

"Aaron," Andie said, cocking her head toward the model.

Joey looked over at him. Their eyes met. He smiled.

"Are you sure you and the Nude Dude aren't—"

"Andie!"

"Okay, okay, don't bite my head off." Andie got out her nearly-finished sketch of Aaron. She scrutinized it. "Even my utter lack of talent can't prevent this guy from looking hot."

She leaned over to look at Joey's sketch. "And you . . . you make him the hottest of all."

"You mean I make him *look* the hottest of all."

"Nuh uh," Andie said, grinning. "I meant exactly what I said."

Chapter 17

"Joey, babe, great legs. Bet Aaron loves 'em."

"Hey, I never knew what you were packin' under those baggy sweaters!"

"Someone get her a tight T-shirt!"

"Nah, get her a tight, *wet* T-shirt. I'll hose you down myself, sweetheart!"

The group of nerdy guys ogled Joey as she walked past them on her way to her locker.

New day, same rumor, Joey thought, hurrying down the hall. Only now the pigskin puppies have evidently passed it on to the audio-visual geeks. Next thing you know, Tolliver Heath will be circulating his latest rendering, namely me and Aaron, up close and personal.

Joey sagged visibly, her hope dashed that the rumor mill had churned out a new partner for Aaron overnight. She walked past the woodworking shop.

"Hey, it's her!" a geeky freshman guy shrieked, running to the door. Three of his friends crowded into the doorway with him as Joey walked by.

"I love you!" the one with glasses yelled.

"I threw out my Pamela Anderson for you!" another yelled. "Your hooters are real!"

"Joey-dot-com! Joey-dot-com! Joey-dot-com!" they all began to chant.

Huh? Joey marched over to the door and was about to ask for an explanation when the shop teacher slammed the door in her face. Swell.

She rounded the corner and stood in front of her locker. Someone had taped a sign to it, covering it from top to bottom. The sign read: THIS IS THE PLACE! HOME OF CAPESIDE'S QUEEN, JOEY.COM!

A couple of guys walked past her. "Yo, Joey-dot-com!" one yelled. "Thanks for making computer lab fun."

Joey just stood there. "Joey-dot-com" meant "Joey.com"?

Were the rumors about her and Aaron actually on the Internet or something? If they were, she was going to kill him. No, she was going to make him go online and deny everything.

And *then* she was going to kill him.

Joey rang Jen's doorbell. She shivered and pulled the sleeves of her oversized sweater over her hands. It looked like rain, and the foreboding sky matched her mood. When she'd arrived home from school, there had been a message from Jen on the answering machine asking her to come over as soon as possible.

"It's an emergency," Jen had said.

Maybe Dawson has more than a cold, Joey worried while she waited for Jen to answer the door. Or maybe Jen and Dawson got back together again last night, and she wants me to hear it from her. Or maybe—

"Josephine," Jen's grandmother said as she opened the door. She wasn't fond of Joey, and she made no bones about it. "Come in. Jennifer is upstairs, she's expecting you."

"Thanks."

"Wipe your feet, please," Grams ordered.

Joey did, then hurried up to Jen's room. She started talking as she opened Jen's door. "Okay, I'm here, and I hope your big emergency is the good kind of emergency."

Jen was sitting in front of her computer. "Good is not exactly the word that comes to mind."

Joey sat down on Jen's bed. She got a terrible, sinking feeling. So it really *was* Jen and Dawson. It had been bound to happen, sooner or later. And Joey knew she had no right to bitch about it.

"Look, let me just take the proverbial bull by the horns here," Joey began. "I'm happy for you. I can't honestly say I'm entirely unaffected by you two getting back together, but if you and Dawson—"

"What are you talking about?"

"You and Dawson." Joey hesitated. "Isn't that what you were talking about?"

"This has nothing to do with Dawson, Joey." Jen beckoned Joey with a crooked finger, then pointed to her computer screen. "Look."

She did. There, filling the screen in all its Technicolor glory, was one of the photos from the La Petite Liz Bette catalog shoot—Joey, in a filmy nightgown that barely reached her thighs, being carried to bed in Aaron's arms.

"I think I'm going to be sick," Joey whispered.

"Might as well save it until you've seen it all, and then you can really barf your guts out." Jen started clicking her mouse. "I'm connected now to some website in Europe. And you're all over it."

Jen was right. Each click of the mouse brought up a different photo of a lingerie-clad Joey on the screen. Sloan was there, too, in some of them.

"So this is Joey-dot-com," Joey said. "Everyone has seen this. Everyone. Turn it off."

Jen did. "I've got the URL bookmarked. Someone sent it to me in an anonymous e-mail. That's how I found it."

"Somebody sent it to you and the entire school," Joey said. She put her face in her hands. "I am so screwed."

Joey felt the bed sag as Jen sat down next to her. "Look, what you did isn't so terrible. You're not the first girl to lie about her age and do soft-core shots so she could make a lot of money fast. You just did it for an online rag instead of getting a staple in your navel. And you thought no one would find out because the online rag was in Europe, am I right?"

"Wait, you think I posed for some online soft-core porn magazine?" Joey yelped.

"Didn't you? Isn't that how you got the money for the Ice House?"

"It was a legit modeling job for a catalog!" Joey

shouted, jumping up. "In fact, it was the ad *you* pointed out to me in the paper!"

"And Aaron just happened to get hired, too?" Joey nodded.

"And *that's* where Pacey met Slow Ann?"

Joey nodded again. "He came with me."

"Well, your legit modeling job turned out to be not so legit, Joey. Because soon the whole world is going to be paying to see a lot more of you online."

"What are you talking about?"

"There's a notice on this website that if you want to see more of Joey and Sloan, you can go to a different web address the day after tomorrow," Jen explained. "That one you pay to visit."

Joey sagged against the wall. "Everyone at school thinks I posed for porno shots. Soon Bessie will know. And the principal. So let's kiss a scholarship to college good-bye. And Dawson. Oh, God—"

She ran into Jen's bathroom and barely got her head over the toilet before she began to throw up. Jen brought her a cold washcloth and put it on the back of her neck. Joey sat on the tile floor, resting her head against the sink, utterly spent. Jen sat on the edge of the bathtub.

Finally, Joey lifted her head, brushing some hair off her sweaty face. "I have a confession to make."

Jen nodded, waiting.

"I have absolutely no idea what to do."

Chapter 18

Dawson's eyes were glued to his TV screen as he watched the end of the video he'd rented, *City of Angels*. He found it touchingly romantic.

Which means if Joey were watching it with me, she'd find it cloyingly sentimental, he thought wryly. Why did she always have to—

There was a rustling at his window. Joey climbed in. She hadn't climbed in in a long time. Dawson's heart sped up with hope. Joey was back.

"Hi" was the brilliance that sprang from his lips.

Joey took in the final frames of the film. "Saw it already—sentimental in the extreme."

"There's nothing wrong with being sentimental. He loves her."

"At the risk of bursting your bubble, Dawson, he's dead. No, wait. He was dead. Now he's alive, and she's dead. I *hate* it when that happens."

"It's possible that true love transcends life and death as we know it," Dawson said.

"Cross-stitch it on a pillow, Dawson, I've got something else on my mind." Joey leaned against his wall. "I suppose you'd like to know to what you owe my unexpected nocturnal visit."

"I have to say, Joey, your attitude has kind of edged out the nostalgia factor," Dawson said. He got up and took the tape out of the VCR, just for something to do. Joey might be back, but clearly not in the way he wanted her back.

"So, how's your cold?" Joey asked.

"My mother plied me with chicken soup. Canned chicken soup. Anything else?"

"How's bodybuilding, then?"

"You came over to ask me that?"

"Okay, so you didn't stick with it," Joey said, shrugging. "Pacey did. Amazing, isn't it?"

"Not really. Pacey will go to frightening lengths to avoid examining anything of real value about his life. Did you come over to talk about Pacey?"

Joey fingered the edge of a large manila envelope in her hands. "No."

"About us, then?" Dawson asked, growing hopeful again.

Joey shook her head.

He sat on his bed again. "Well, then, it seems to be we've reached the age and time in our relationship such as it is—"

"Such as it isn't," Joey corrected.

Dawson hesitated. "Isn't," he agreed finally. "Which seems all the more reason that the beginnings of our conversations take on a somewhat more conventional form. You know, you pick up the phone and call me. You ask if you might drop by—"

"I couldn't—"

"Or tomorrow," Dawson continued, barely keeping the edge out of his voice. It beat giving in to the hurt of her rejection, that was for sure. "Tomorrow is a very interesting concept. You could have called me and asked me if we might have this little chat tomorrow."

Joey dropped the manila envelope at her feet. "Don't you think that if I could have waited until tomorrow, I would have, Dawson?"

He looked down at the envelope. "What's that?"

Joey looked down, too. She had been planning just to leave the envelope there and escape, so she wouldn't have to face him. But she knew she had to, eventually. It was just so humiliating.

"Joey? Are you okay?" He went to her, because she suddenly looked as if she was going to cry.

Wordlessly she bent down to pick up the envelope and thrust it at him. "Before you open that, I just want to say—"

"What?" He reached for her hand. "Look, whatever it is, Joey, we can work it out."

"Everything can't be 'worked out,' Dawson, though I know that must come as something of a shock to your Disneyesque view of the universe." She took her hand back. "Just open it."

He did.

And looked at shot after shot of Joey in sexy lingerie, which Jen had downloaded off her computer. Six of them were different poses of her with Aaron

Poole—either being carried to bed in his arms or already in bed with him.

Dawson's face grew steely. A vein began to pulse in his forehead. His chin jutted forward. Finally, he put all the photos back in the envelope and silently handed them back to her.

Then he turned his back on her and began getting his stuff together for school the next morning, as if she just wasn't there.

"You aren't known for your brooding silences," Joey noted nervously.

Wordlessly, he got the tape of *City of Angels* and threw it in his backpack so he could return it to ScreenPlay the next day.

"Maybe you could borrow a few words from your usual overanalytic verbosity," Joey joked self-consciously. "I'm sure there will be more than enough left for your next—"

"What is it that you want, Joey?"

She was taken aback. "Well, to talk about this."

"Why? Is it some bizarre attempt to make me jealous? Not that the concept makes any sense, Joey, because, as you love to remind me, you're the one who left me. So that lets jealousy out."

"I wasn't trying to—"

"I'm standing here looking at you, Joey, and it's like I don't even know you at all. Who is the desperate, pathetic, shallow girl in those photos? And what deep-seated insecurity made her pose for them?"

Joey's face burned with anger and hurt. "For your information, Dawson, those photos are from a modeling job I did, for a perfectly legitimate catalog. I got paid. A lot. I did it so Bessie could get the pipes fixed in the Ice House, so we could eat, pay our bills, and not lose our house. I was Bessie's secret angel, isn't that a riot? And I didn't tell you because I knew you'd be the self-righteous butthole that you're being right now."

Silence. Through the open window, the first katydids of spring were croaking. Neither of them noticed.

"Did the model from your Advanced Life Drawing class get you the job?" Dawson finally asked.

"No. I had no idea he'd be there. It was one of those bizarre coincidences that don't seem like they could be, but are. Look, these photos were only supposed to be in this catalog, and the catalog was only supposed to come out in Europe," Joey continued. "But somehow they got put on the Internet, and just about everyone at school has seen them. If you hadn't been out with a cold, you'd know about it already."

"Do you mean to tell me that all those pituitary cases on the football team have drooled over these?" Dawson asked.

"Them and everyone else," Joey said. She slid down the wall and sat on the rug. Suddenly, she was exhausted.

"You're kidding me. How could you?"

She looked up at him. "You just don't get it, do you? Your roughest problem is worrying about whether your dad is going to move back home or not. You have no idea what it's like to wonder if you're even going to *have* a home."

"Joey, I—"

She got up. "You know how I loathe melodrama, Dawson, so this might be a good time for me to exit. I only have two more things to say to you. One, I don't have to answer to you; and two, I didn't do anything wrong." She had one foot out the window when she turned back to him. "Make that three things, and the third thing is this—"

An ache began in the back of her throat.

"Don't you ever, *ever* lecture me about love again, Dawson, because you don't know the meaning of the word."

She climbed down the ladder, tears coursing down her cheeks. When she got to the ground, she brushed them away with the sleeve of her sweater and took off for the creek. There was her boat, outlined in the moonlight. She wished she could row it into someone else's life.

"Joey! Joey!"

She turned around. Dawson was running toward her.

"I'm glad I caught you," he said, breathing hard.

"Don't you know that too many false endings diffuse a movie's emotional impact?" Joey asked.

"I just wanted to say that I understand," Dawson said between breaths. "Why you did what you did, I mean."

She folded her arms. "Is that it?"

"And I'm sorry that everyone at school knows. Did anyone say anything to you?"

"We're talking about Capeside High, Dawson," Joey reminded him. "What do you think?"

"I think . . . you're going to need a friend tomorrow. I want you to know that you can count on me."

"As Slow Ann would say, 'Wow.' Big of you, Dawson."

She turned to get into the boat, but Dawson's hand on her arm stopped her. Gently, he turned her to him. His eyes sought out hers in the moonlight. "I want you to know something else, too. About how I reacted. Overreacted. Didn't give you a chance to—"

"Cut to the chase, Dawson."

"I'm sorry. That's what I wanted to say. I'm sorry, Joey."

Stupid tears. Why did they always come when she wanted them the least? The next thing she knew, Dawson's arms were around her, hugging her to him.

"I'm such an idiot, Joey," he whispered into her hair. "I almost forgot the most important thing of all."

"What?"

"It's always been you and me against the world, Joey. And it still is. It still is."

On the other side of town, Pacey stood in front of the mirror in Deputy Doug's gym, striking muscle poses and checking out his reflection.

"You look like a weenie," he told his reflection. "Correction, a skinny, weenie imbecile who has gained a grand total of one and a half pounds of lean, mean muscle, proving yet again that you are, now and forever, Pacey Witter, Born Loser."

He bowed mockingly to his reflection, and his

stomach gurgled painfully. The combination of Car-boGas and supplements was wreaking havoc with his intestines. He was constantly making up excuses to get himself out of whatever room he was in, so that he could pass gas in private.

Maybe it was the buffalo liver extracts.

"Figures," he muttered. "Deputy Doug downs the swill, he gets muscles. I down it, I get gas."

He looked at his watch and realized it was past the time when he had said he'd call Sloan. She liked him to call her every night, so she could tell him every minute, excruciating detail of her day. Now the thought of facing one more of those phone calls filled him with dread.

He had to face it. Dawson and Joey and Jen were right. Sloan was mind-bogglingly, teeth-shatteringly dumb. And boring. And self-involved.

On the other hand, she was beyond hot to look at. Being seen with her had been great. How much of a loser could he be, if a girl who looked like that was out with him?

But the truth was, he missed Andie. Big time. He missed her mind, her banter, even her jokes at his expense.

And Andie was beautiful, too. Not in that fantasy centerfold kind of way, maybe. But Andie's kind of beauty left Sloan in the dust. "Careful, Pace," he warned himself out loud. "That was way too mature of a thought." He slid down the wall.

He couldn't very well try to get Andie back when he was seeing Sloan. Which meant he had to tell Sloan it was over.

No time like the present.

He reached for the phone, but it rang before he had a chance to punch in her number.

"Talk to me," he barked into the phone.

"Pacey? It's me, Sloan. You were supposed to call me fifteen minutes ago. No, wait. Sixteen minutes ago."

"No kidding? Maybe my watch stopped," Pacey said. "Listen, before you tell me what you did today, we need to talk."

"Oh, wow, you read my mind. It's like you're psycho or something!" Sloan exclaimed.

"Do you mean *psychic?*" Pacey asked carefully.

Sloan giggled into the phone. "It was a joke, silly! Get it? Psycho, psychic?"

"Wow." He paced with the phone.

Just tell her, you wuss, he commanded himself. Right now.

"Pacey?"

"Oh, sorry, you caught me between stomach crunches." He took a deep breath, about to blow off the best-looking girl he was likely ever to get in his life. "Listen, Sloan, you are a really great girl—"

"You think?" Sloan interrupted eagerly.

"I do. Just, you know, great. But there's this other girl, her name is Andie. Actually, she's the one who came into the Bowl-a-Rama that night—"

"Wait, wait, Pacey?" Sloan called. "Can you tell me about her after I say what I have to say? Because I'm afraid I'll lose my nerve, and also I really have to pee."

"Oh, sure, go ahead," Pacey said.

"Well, here's the thing. I can't go out with you

anymore," Sloan said. "I'm really sorry to hurt your feelings like this. I hope we can stay friends."

Pacey's mouth gaped open. *She* was dropping *him*? Had she not heard a word he was saying about Andie? But what difference did it make? Why make her feel bad?

"Gee, Sloan, if that's how you feel," he said.

"Wow, this is, like, really hard for me," Sloan went on earnestly. "I mean, you're super-sweet, Pacey. The thing is, I'm looking for someone a little . . . deeper."

Deeper? This had to be a joke. Either Jen or Joey, or even Andie, had to be impersonating Sloan. And he had fallen for it. What a chump he was!

"Real funny," Pacey said into the phone. "Excellent vocal likeness. I almost fell for it. Deeper. Ha."

"Wow, I guess you're so hurt that you're kind of like not making any sense," Sloan continued. "My astrologer says I should be with a guy who is more my cosmic soul-mate."

Now Pacey wasn't sure if it really was Sloan or not. "What shape is the birthmark on your butt?" he asked quickly.

"I told you before, a rosebud. It's so small that it looks like a zit in photos, though. I told you that, too."

Oh, God. It really *was* Sloan.

"I know you're really into working out and everything," Sloan went on, "but lately I've been thinking a lot about the meaning of life and all that. And, also, I'm a fire sign, and you're a water. That really puts out my spirit."

"Uh-huh" was all Pacey could muster.

"Did you want to say anything, Pacey?"

"Gee, can't think of a thing."

Sloan hesitated; something in her voice changed. "Look, I know I'm no Cindy Crawford, okay? She was like this honor student in college. I'm not even ever going to get to college. Who am I kidding, I didn't even finish high school."

For the first time, something about Sloan truly touched Pacey. He just had no idea what to do about it.

"I'm not so dumb that I don't know that people make fun of me sometimes," she went on. "But you know what, Pacey? That doesn't mean I don't think about deep things."

"No, it doesn't," Pacey agreed. He had a very un-Pacey-like feeling. Regret. That he had ever been one of those people who had made fun of her lack of brains.

"Are you there, Pacey?"

"You're not dumb. Sloan," Pacey said firmly. "I'm sorry if . . . anyone ever made you feel that way."

"Thanks. I hope you have a wonderful life, Pacey. Oh, wow, before I go, there's something I really want to share with you. It's very meaningful to me."

"Sure, Sloan. What is it?"

"There's this great book, *Jonathan Livingston Seagull.* I read it this week, and it changed my life. It was, like, wow. So you should read it, too. Okay? So, anyway, good luck, Pacey Buffman. Stay the sweetheart you are."

Sloan hung up, and Pacey was left holding the phone, a dial tone ringing in his ear.

Chapter 19

By the next day, the football team had made certain that anyone at Capeside High who had not heard of Joey.com was now well informed. Someone had printed up little cards and stuck them in the boys' gym lockers: FOR A GOOD TIME, CALL JOEY. COM. Also on the cards was the exact URL address where Joey's lingerie pictures could be found.

Joey's life was, quite simply, hell. Everywhere she went, she was ogled at, smirked about, and pointed to. Pacey, her partner in crime, was no help. When she got a chance to talk with him at lunch, he was too busy crowing about his reunion with Andie to put any focus on Joey.

"What about Slow Ann?" Joey had asked him.

"I've hired a hypnotist to erase her from my memory," Pacey had claimed, then added "Wow" as he hurried off to meet Andie.

If there was a silver lining to the day, it was that the Joey.com scandal hadn't attracted any attention from teachers or administrators. They were all too busy hyperventilating over a dispute that had begun weeks earlier, when a senior girl had come to school with a midriff-baring top that exposed her navel ring. The principal wanted to ban midriffs *and* navel rings, but certain teachers like Ms. Lewinger said banning midriffs and navel rings was just another scheme to keep students powerless.

Students and parents were coming down on one side or the other. That morning, the principal had issued a de facto ban, which had caused the drama teacher to expose *her* navel ring to her first period class in protest.

The navel ring hysteria fully occupied the school administration—thank God for small favors—but Joey.com had instantly replaced it as the scandal of the day. Some little freshman girl even came up to Joey at lunch and said her friend had told her that Joey was a prostitute, and was it true, and how much money did Joey make, and wasn't she worried about AIDS?

All day long, Joey did her best to hold her head up high. But it was tough. Dawson seemed to show up everywhere she went. She knew he was doing it to be nice, but hearing people say that stuff in front of him was worse than hearing it alone, so she finally asked him to take a hike. Please.

"I see you lived to tell the tale," Andie said to Joey as Joey slid into her seat in Advanced Life Drawing class. "What's it like to be infamous?"

"It sucks, so let's talk about something else," Joey

said, getting out her charcoal. "I hear you and Buff-man are once again an item."

"Buffman?"

"The former Pacey Witter, transformed into Abs of Steel a.k.a. Buff Man," Joey translated.

"Abs of mush is more like it," Andie snorted. "But what can I say, they're my abs of mush."

Two guys across the room looked over at Joey, one said something she couldn't hear, and then they both laughed uproariously.

"Do you realize they're picturing you naked right now?" Andie asked Joey.

Joey slammed down her sketch pad. "Thank you so much, Andie, that's very helpful. What happened with Sloan and Pacey, anyway?"

"Who? The model?" Andie shrugged. "Pacey decided he wanted me and not her—can you blame him?—and I decided space was highly overrated. Where's the Nude Dude?"

Joey looked up. Aaron was missing from his perch.

"So what was it like," Andie asked eagerly, "to be in Aaron's arms? He's hardly wearing any clothes, you're in a flimsy teddie, you can feel the manly muscles of his—"

"Just out of curiosity, do you read really bad romance novels before you go to sleep?" Joey asked.

"Dish not," Andie said solemnly. "*Gone With the Wind* is a romance novel. So, does Bessie know you did those photos?"

"Posed for a catalog," Joey corrected. "And the answer is no."

"She's the only person in Capeside who doesn't, then."

"Very funny." Joey sighed and rubbed a finger over a stray line of charcoal. "I know I have to tell her, before she finds out from someone else. What fun."

"And Dawson?"

"I told him last night. He's been following me around all day like some really bad remake of *My Bodyguard*."

Andie grinned. "And they say chivalry is dead."

Ms. Lewinger walked into the room with Aaron. He snuck a quick sympathetic glance at Joey and then took his place on the platform in the center of the studio.

Andie leaned close to Joey. "Your paramour arrives."

Joey shot her a deadly look.

"Hey, I just wanted to tell you that you looked really beautiful in those photos, Joey," Andie said. "Seriously. If I looked like that in lingerie, I'd—"

"Oh, great." Joey slumped down in her seat.

"What?" Andie asked.

Joey looked significantly out the open classroom door. Dawson was standing there. Just . . . standing there.

Ms. Lewinger closed the door and began to talk about some artist named Chuck Close and his influence on neo-realism.

Andie could still see Dawson through the glass pane of the door. "He must have cut his last class to wait for you. That's so sweet."

"That's so Dawson," Joey muttered.

*   *   *

Dawson paced outside Joey's art class. He checked his watch one more time. Any second now, the class would let out, and students would stream through the door. Except, he figured, Joey. She always seemed to stay after class at least a few minutes. She *said* it was because she got so wrapped up in her drawing.

And I believed her, Dawson thought bitterly. But it was really Joey and that sleazy pornographic male model hanging out together after everyone left. That must have been when he hit on her and talked her into doing those sleazy photos. Played on her worries about money. Seduced her with his perfect pecs and his movie-star smile and his—

Kids began to explode out the door of the art room. Andie walked by him and waved. Jen tried to talk with him, but he blew her off—he'd have to explain it to her later.

Finally, Ms. Lewinger hurried out, followed by Aaron. Joey was still in there. Perfect.

Dawson followed Aaron as he headed to the side doors of the school, the ones closest to the parking lot. Just before Aaron got out the door, Dawson tapped him on the shoulder. Aaron turned around.

"Were you under the impression that you could do anything you want and there wouldn't be any consequences?" Dawson demanded.

"Excuse me?" Aaron asked. "Do I know you?"

"Dawson Leery. I'm Joey's best friend. You've made her life miserable, do you even recognize that? Or are you too infatuated with yourself to have bothered to think about her at all?"

"What are you talking about?"

Dawson could feel anger flushing his face. "I'm talking about how you seduced Joey into doing those pornographic shots with you."

"First of all, those are modeling photos from a catalog shoot, not pornography," Aaron snapped. "Second, I had nothing to do with her getting the job. And third, Joey seems to have both a mind and a mouth of her own, so I don't really understand what this little confrontation is about."

That did it. Before Dawson could even think about what he was doing, he had grabbed Aaron by his T-shirt.

"Hey!" Aaron protested.

"Now it's my turn," Dawson said, holding fast to Aaron's shirt. "You may be in significantly better shape than I am, but I assure you that right now my fury outweighs your muscle. Whether or not you got this job for Joey, you certainly knew she was under age. Which means you could have stopped all this before it started."

"Lots of models are under age," Aaron said, his voice low and even. "How did I know that her parents hadn't signed the contract for her?"

Dawson's eyes bored into his. "Your flimsy excuses may allow you to look in the mirror in the morning, but they don't work with me. You can't stand there and tell me that you didn't love having Joey in your arms, didn't love having her in bed with you—"

"You think I'm hitting on your girlfriend, is that what this is about? I *have* a girlfriend."

"Guys like you want to seduce every great-looking girl they can get their hands on."

Aaron carefully removed Dawson's fist from his shirt. "Joey and I were acting," Aaron said. "Get it? Acting? Let me give you a little unsolicited advice, Dawson. Joey is a beautiful girl. You'd better check out that insecurity thing you've got going on, or else you're gonna lose her, man."

Red fury filled Dawson's eyes. Of all the condescending, patronizing . . . He grabbed Aaron's shirt again, harder this time. His fist went back of its own volition; he aimed for Aaron's perfectly chiseled nose—

"Dawson, what the hell are you doing?" Joey yelled, running over to them.

Aaron grasped Dawson's arm and yanked down. Hard. Dawson's fist fell to his side.

"We seem to be fighting over a girl," Aaron said ironically. "Actually, he seems to be fighting, while I seem to be trying to keep myself from fighting back."

Joey turned on Dawson. "Are you out of your mind?"

"What kind of a friend would I be if I just let him use you, Joey?"

"He didn't *use* me! No one *used* me."

"Aaron? What is going on?" The young woman with the lilting Jamaican accent had just come in from outside. She had caramel-colored skin, short dreadlocked hair, and a muscular, voluptuous body—easily a size fourteen. Her face was pleasant, but hardly beautiful in any traditional sense.

Aaron immediately wrapped his arms around her, hugging her close. "What is going on is too crazy to explain." He turned to Dawson. "This is my girl-friend, Sashia—she's in her last year of pre-law."

He nodded at Joey. "That's the girl I told you about who did the modeling job with me." He looked over at Dawson. "And that's . . . I'm not quite sure who or what that is."

Sashia nodded at them. "Lovely to meet you both." She took Aaron's hand. "We're late to get student tickets to *A Midsummer Night's Dream*," she reminded him. "Let's go."

"Nice strutting and fretting with you," Aaron said to Dawson, as he headed toward the exit with Sashia. He pointed a finger at Dawson. "Hate me all you want, but remember what I told you."

They disappeared out the door.

Joey turned on Dawson. "Were you under some delusion that it was your job to fight my battles for me?"

"I know you can take care of yourself, Joey. Credit me with a little knowledge about your general capacity for self-protection. Friends don't allow other people to hurt their friends. Not without putting up a fight."

Joey sighed and ran her hand through her hair wearily.

"Try to let this sink into your frontal lobes, Dawson. Aaron did not hurt me. He did not get me the modeling job."

"But don't you see that he—"

"Reality check, Dawson. You didn't almost attempt to pound Aaron just now because you think he hurt me, you did it because he threatens you. A guy like Aaron brings out the worst in you, Dawson.

You assume that he's as shallow and stupid and self-involved as Slow Ann because that's what you need him to be. Well, guess what? Your pain is not more noble than anyone else's."

He stood there, stunned, as Joey turned and walked away. But then she turned back to him. "By the way, Gérard Depardieu is not going to play you in *The Dawson Leery Story*. This is real life, Dawson. When you decide to come out from behind the lens and admit it, we can talk.

"Until then," she added, "just leave me alone."

Chapter 20

Joey and Jen stood in front of an old stone building, carefully restored, in downtown Boston. Joey looked at a brass plate on the wall of the building. "Alanzo Bartkevicius," she read aloud nervously. "That's him. I admit it, I'm impressed that you managed to get us an appointment with him overnight."

"As my often ethically challenged mother loves to say, if you're going to fight, you may as well fight dirty."

They went into the lobby and pressed the elevator button. "So, what does fighting dirty entail, exactly?" Joey asked, looping some hair behind her ear. "When I called and tried to make an appointment to see him, his secretary sniffed that he was booked until the turn of the century, and I think she meant the next century."

"I just mentioned to his rottweiler of a secretary

that two people from *People* were terribly interested in meeting with Alan. Funny how she turned into a poodle in a split second."

Joey laughed. "That was brilliant."

They got on the elevator. "When you grow up in New York City, you learn to work the system." They got off on the fifth floor and went through the heavy oak door to Alan's offices. The waiting area had a Southwestern motif, right down to skulls of bulls as centerpieces on the two coffee tables. Various famous and unknown models' magazine covers graced the walls, all expensively framed.

The secretary's desk was empty.

Joey bit at a hangnail. She was so nervous. After her run-in with Dawson the day before, Joey had found Jen waiting for her in the parking lot. It seemed that Jen had come up with a plan. She laid it out for Joey, who had to admit it was better than anything she had come up with.

Step one, though, was getting an appointment with Alan. That had seemed impossible. But Jen had done it. So one day and one long bus ride later, here they were.

A bone-thin young woman with very short jet-black hair and thigh-high boots strode in from the back hall. "Yes?" she asked when she saw them.

"Hi," Jen said. "We're from *People*. We've got the five forty-five with Alan."

"Oh, yes!" she said, her eyes lighting up. "I'll let him know you're here." She pressed a button on her phone, then spoke into it.

"Alan, your five forty-five is here. From *People*," she added significantly before she hung up. "I'll take you right back to him. Can I get you anything? Coffee? Coke? Water?"

"Evian," Jen ordered imperiously.

The girl's face fell. "We only have Calistoga."

"Please," Jen scoffed dismissively.

As the girl led them down the hallway, Joey looked over at Jen. "Evian?" she mouthed.

"My mother also always says, the bitchier you are, the more they respect you," Jen explained, her voice low.

The secretary opened yet another heavy door and ushered them into Alan's office. Alan was looking at some contact sheets through a loop.

"Mr. Bartkevicius?" Jen asked.

Alan looked up. He gave Joey a long, puzzled look, as if trying to place her face. When it dawned on him who she was, a bemused smile crossed his face. "Josephine. And to think I fell for the *People* magazine scam. If I didn't like you, I would be very irritated."

Anger surged through Joey. *"You'd* be angry with—"

Jen squeezed Joey's arm hard, which clearly was a signal for Joey to shut up. "Mr. Bartkevicius, I'm Jennifer Lindley. Can we sit down? We need to talk."

Alan waved the two of them toward his taupe leather sofa. He sat in a tweedy oversized chair, his chin in his hand. "Your turn," he told Jen. "Though I can't imagine what you two might want."

"No, my turn," Joey said before Jen could open her mouth. It was bad enough that Jen Lindley had seen the photos of her and that Jen was the one who had gotten this appointment, but she was not about to have Jen fight her battles for her, too.

"Those pictures that you took of me," Joey began, her heart pounding, "they weren't just for the catalog in France, were they? Because they ended up on the Internet."

"I imagine they did," Alan said easily. "So?"

"So people I know saw them. You told me they were for a catalog in France. Which means you put those photos on the Internet without my permission."

He tapped one finger against his lips. "That's what this little drama is all about?"

Joey nodded.

"Josephine, *I* did not put your photos on the Internet. I assure you that *I* have much better things to do with my time. The catalog company put your photos on their website. They paid you a great deal of money, they own the photos, they are trying to sell their lingerie online. Now, is the mystery cleared up for you, dear?"

Joey crossed her arms, glaring at him. "I never gave permission to put my photos on the Internet."

"You most certainly did," Alan replied. "You signed a contract which allows La Petite Liz Bette to use the photos of you in any medium. It's standard, it's perfectly aboveboard, and it's legal."

"Not if she's a minor, it isn't," Jen said smugly.

Joey pulled a folded-up piece of paper out of her back pocket, unfolded it, and handed it to Alan.

He looked up after reading it, and for the first time since they'd entered his office, he looked angry.

"Well, it seems that you're not even close to eighteen, Josephine. You lied to me. That is fraud."

"She's not the one who'll get into trouble, though," Jen said quickly. "You will."

"Yes, I most certainly will," he agreed. He handed Joey back her birth certificate. "Am I smelling an ugly little blackmail plan here, ladies? You'll claim that you never told me you were eighteen unless I do . . . whatever it is you want. Make you a star, get you a cover, get you dinner with Donald Trump. I'm deeply disappointed in you, Josephine."

"We're not blackmailing you," Joey said. She felt bad. She liked Alan. "I'm sorry I lied to you about my age. I needed the money for a . . . a serious family emergency."

"I see." Alan sighed, making a tent with his fingers. "This is how you paid for your abortion."

"Not that," Joey said.

"Please, Josephine, don't think that because I'm gay I don't understand about—"

"I didn't get pregnant," Joey insisted. "Look, my parents are . . . gone. My sister owns a restaurant, and the stupid pipes burst. We needed the money to fix them, or we would have lost everything, okay? So I'm sorry I had to lie to you to get the job, but I'm not sorry I got it." She sat back on the couch, furious. She hadn't intended to tell him the details of her sad, little life.

"You could have gotten me into a tremendous amount of trouble, Josephine." Alan sharpened the already knifelike crease in his perfect Ralph Lauren pants. "You could still sue me."

"I won't sue you," Joey assured him. "All I want is to have my photos taken off the Internet."

He reached for the lucite phone on the coffee table in front of him. "It's midnight in Paris," he said as he began to punch digits into the phone. "They're going to have my head for this. But better me than you.

"Hello?" Alan said into the phone, *"Christophe? C'est Alan."*

He had a long conversation with someone in rapid, perfect French—Jen, who'd taken French at her private school back in New York, could barely follow it, except that Alan kept saying *"Je suis vraiment désolé"*—that he was extremely sorry—repeatedly. Then he hung up the phone.

Joey and Jen stared at him, waiting.

"Christophe said to wait ten minutes and then log on to the Internet," Alan told them. "Your photos will be gone. They'll send the negatives to me by overnight courier. You can come pick them up the day after tomorrow, if you like. La Petite Liz Bette can no longer use them for any reason."

"What if they don't do it?" Joey asked.

"They'll do it," Jen answered for him. "Because they're still afraid that you'll sue, Joey."

"So young and yet so savvy," Alan said dryly. "You're quite right. And while you are a lovely young—very *young*—girl, Josephine, you are worth neither the time, energy, nor expense of a lawsuit."

"I appreciate that you called them for me," Joey said, her voice low.

Alan stood up. "Do me a favor, Josephine. Don't pull anything like this again." He held out his hand.

She got up and shook it. He really was a nice man. And she really had lied to him.

"I just want to apologize to you. And . . . and if you want the money back, I can pay you back. Not right away. And it will have to be on a payment plan. But I'll pay back every—"

Alan waved her off. "Believe me, to Christophe, it is not even a decimal point in his books. He said to keep it. He doesn't want the hassle." He walked Joey and Jen to the door. "Next time, Josephine, get your parents to—"

And then he remembered—she'd said her parents were gone.

"Well, that was particularly gauche of me," he said. "I apologize."

Joey reached for the doorknob, then hesitated. "You are a really nice man, Mr. Bartkevicius. I just wanted to tell you that."

"Thank you." He smiled at her. Then he reached into the inside pocket of his suit jacket and pulled out four tickets to something. "As a parting peace offer, these are passes to a fashion show and party at Trash, that hot new club in Roxbury, on Saturday night. A number of my models are in the show, so I'm loaded with comps."

Joey raised her eyebrows, and Alan laughed. "No, you don't have to be eighteen to enter. No alcohol."

"Thanks, then," Joey said, taking the passes. "Bye."

He opened the door for them and held it, smiling at her kindly. "I wish you only good things, Josephine. Good luck with the pipes."

Chapter 21

"You did *what*?" Joey asked Jen. She craned her neck around to look at Jen, who was in the backseat.

"She invited Dawson, what's the biggie?" Andie asked as she turned her car down Dawson's street.

"Alan gave us four tickets to this thing," Jen reminded Joey. "You invited Pacey, he said he was busy—"

"If it turns out he was busy with that model, he's toast," Andie put in.

"—which meant we had an extra ticket," Jen continued. "It seemed ridiculous to waste it."

"The only person you could think of to invite in all of Capeside was Dawson Leery?" Joey asked. Her tone was very dubious.

"Well, I could have asked Grams to get down and funky with us," Jen said sarcastically.

"Hey, this is my idea of a good time," Andie said. She pulled the car up Dawson's driveway. "The two of you and Dawson are like some really adolescent soap opera. It's like I know it's stupid, but I keep watching anyway."

She honked her horn. Dawson came out. Wordlessly, he got into the backseat next to Jen. Andie pulled the car back onto the street as Joey turned to glare at him. She hadn't spoken to him since he'd almost assaulted Aaron Poole at school.

"And to what do we owe the pleasure of Dawson Leery attending an event as shallow as a fashion bash?" Joey asked him.

"You owe it to Jen's inviting me," Dawson said evenly. "And to my saying yes."

"Well, then, it worked out nicely that you're sitting back there together," Joey said.

"I think so," Dawson agreed.

Joey turned back around, her face a mask of cold fury. She pushed Andie's Barenaked Ladies cassette in and turned it up full blast.

"We're having some fun now, campers!" Andie yelled. "Ya-hoo!" She sang along at the top of her lungs, all the way to Roxbury.

"Gotta get gas," Andie said, pulling up to the full-service pump at the Chevron station just off the highway exit for Roxbury. She knew Roxbury was a somewhat diccy neighborhood and wanted to make as few stops there as possible.

"Since we're splitting the gas money, you could have gone self-serve," Joey pointed out.

"And miss one of the few remaining quasi-idle

rich moments of my young life?" Andie asked. "I bet Jen will never pump her own gas."

"Of course I will, that's ridiculous," Jen defended herself. Sometimes Andie really irritated Jen.

"And now we know how Jen got rich," Andie said lightly.

"Please. I'm going to the ladies room." Jen got out and slammed the door.

"Fill 'er up," Andie told the station attendant who appeared at her window. She looked over at Joey. "Jen's insulted, huh?"

"Huh," Joey agreed.

"I guess that means I should go do that female bonding thing with her in the john," Andie sighed. "But it's just way too *My So-Called Life* for my taste. Wish me luck." She got out and went after Jen anyway.

In the car, Dawson and Joey were as silent as they had been on the entire ride.

Finally, Dawson cleared his throat. "It feels very strange to have this heavy silence between us, Joey."

She stared straight ahead.

"And awkward," Dawson went on. "And wrong. Look, I may not have made the best choice with Aaron the other day—"

Now she turned to him. "Did that significant insight just dawn on you, Dawson? It's a classic movie moment: The Antihero's Epiphany at the Full-Service Pump."

"That'll be fifteen bucks even," the attendant said into the open window. Wordlessly, Dawson took the money out of his wallet and handed it over. Joey got four dollars out of the back pocket of her jeans and handed it to him.

"Split four ways means I owe you a quarter change."

She shook her head. "I am not that desperate, thank you very much."

"I'm not saying you don't have a right to be angry with me," Dawson said doggedly. "But I think you're missing something significant here, Joey. I have a right to be angry with you, too."

"I told you, those photos have nothing to do with—"

"I know that," Dawson said. "That's not what I meant."

"So, what did you mean, then?"

Dawson stared out the window. "When someone is your friend, your best friend, you like to think that she trusts you. And it hurts to find out she doesn't, that she confided it Pacey instead of you—"

"But you wouldn't have understood, Dawson—"

"That she assumes you wouldn't understand without even giving you a chance to understand. That she would let someone take photos of her that she doesn't feel good about, rather than let that friend ask his mom for a loan."

Joey was silent for a long time. "We can't pretend that everything that happened between us didn't happen. And that means that our friendship can never be what it was before . . . whatever it is that happened . . . happened."

"I know."

Now she turned to him. "I knew just how you feel about modeling, and how shallow that whole physical beauty thing is. There were no emotional strings with Pacey."

Dawson nodded.

"And I could never, ever have let you ask your mom for a loan for me," Joey went on. "You know I couldn't."

Dawson leaned forward and put his hand on hers. "Let's assume for the moment that everything you said is true, Joey. You still decided it all on your own without sharing any of it with me. It felt safer to you. But it just feels sad to me."

"We're ba-ack!" Andie sang out, opening the car door. Jen got in the backseat. Dawson took his hand off Joey's and sat back, but not before Jen noticed.

"Did you two kiss and make up?" Jen asked Dawson sharply.

"We kept our lips to ourselves," Joey replied.

"I paid for the gas," Dawson told Andie.

"Then we're outta here." Andie pulled out of the station. "Lucky Dawson. Out with three gorgeous babes."

They easily found the club: a huge neon logo of a garbage can with tattooed arms and legs sticking out of it blinked TRASH on and off. Andie managed to squeeze into a tiny spot in the packed parking lot, and the four of them showed their comp passes to the enormous bouncer and went inside.

The rock music was so loud, it felt as if the whole room was vibrating. Recessed amber spotlights created a golden glow on the huge, dimly lit room. The deejay's perch was high above the dance floor, and there were large pedestals of various heights on which people danced, mostly great-looking, skimpily clad girls. Other people danced on the part of the dance floor not covered by the runway.

"Tickets?" A cute guy in a tuxedo jacket and no shirt took the four comp passes from Joey. Then he moved a velvet rope so that they could go onto the dance floor.

"*Hullabaloo*," Jen said, watching a girl in a white fringed minidress dancing by herself on one of the pedestals.

"What?" Joey asked, yelling over the music.

"It was some old TV show where girls danced on pedestals," Jen explained. "My mom was on it. Every time she got really depressed, she forced me to sit down and watch it with her, so she could get even more depressed about the good old days before crow's feet and my father entered her life."

The music changed to something slow. Jen looked over at Dawson. "Dance?" Dawson hesitated.

"It's just a dance, Dawson," Jen said, matter-of-factly. "It doesn't commit you, so feel free to take a deep, pain-free breath."

"I'd love to dance with you, Jen." He took her hand and led her to the dance floor.

"They do look cute together, you have to admit," Andie said to Joey.

"Consider it admitted, Andie."

Andie looked around. "Major talent here. That guy at the door in the tux jacket—"

"Uh-huh." Joey's eyes were glued to Jen and Dawson, as they swayed in each other's arms.

"And I'm pretty sure that Leonardo DiCaprio and Matt Damon just walked in, stark naked," Andie went on. "Yep, that's them, all right."

Joey tore her eyes from Dawson and Jen. "Did you say something?"

"Let me ask you a question, Joey. I'm really curious about this. If you still have it so bad for Dawson, why are you over here when he's over there?"

"I don't still have it so bad for Dawson."

"And it didn't bother me to see Pacey with that model chick," Andie replied. "Yuh, right."

The music's volume dropped even lower as a voice came over the sound system. "Ladies and gentlemen, if you'd take seats for the fashion bash, we'll be starting in five minutes."

Dawson and Jen joined Andie and Joey, and then, along with the rest of the crowd, they found seats. Soon the lights dimmed even further, and a spotlight hit the microphone set up at the end of the runway. A gorgeous woman in her thirties, wearing a drop-dead silver gown, came out from the curtained area behind the runway. Some people applauded.

"Thank you very much," she said into the mike, her voice low and sexy. A few photographers snapped her photo, flashbulbs popped. "I'm Alicia O'Brien, and tonight I'm very excited to introduce a wonderful new designer to you. He hails from right here in Roxbury and that is why he wanted to launch his collection here tonight. So, with no further introduction, I present to you the first collection of Mr. D'Wayne Eaton!"

Retro disco music began to thump through the sound system. Donna Summers wailed "She Works Hard for the Money" as the curtains parted, and female models began to strut down the runway. The first girl had electric red hair streaked purple. She wore a silver Lurex teddie with oversized silver sunglasses and glitter-filled silver platform shoes. All the models that followed wore silver lingerie, some made entirely out of painted feathers.

"Hey, isn't that Sloan?" Joey asked, peering up at a silver-haired girl.

"Yeah, wow, you're right," Jen agreed. "Small world and all that."

Andie scrutinized Sloan in the leather bikini. "I don't know what Pacey saw in her," she sniffed. "I mean, I could buy a chest like that at my friendly neighborhood plastic surgeon's any time I wanted to."

"Please don't," Joey said. "Fakes are so gross."

Now the music changed to "It's Raining Men" by the Weathergirls. The curtain opened boldly, and a gorgeous guy wearing black silk pajama bottoms covered in silver stars sashayed down the runway.

"Now we're talking!" Andie whooped, whistling at him. It's about time.

Dawson looked at his watch. He had zero interest in a fashion show, and less than zero interest now that they'd switched over to male models.

"What do you think, Dawson, can you picture yourself in that?" Jen teased.

Dawson looked up. The model had on a black and red paisley silk smoking jacket, with a pipe in his mouth.

"I would look like an idiot in that," Dawson said.

Jen laughed. "You're right, you would."

"Only guys in old British pictures could ever carry that kind of thing off," Andie was saying, only half watching the runway. "American men are way too—"

"Omigod!" Jen shrieked, literally jumping out of her seat. She pointed at the runway. "That's Pacey!"

Andie, Dawson, and Joey jumped up, too. Their jaws hung open. Because strutting down the runway in black boxers with silver racing stripes was the Buff Man himself. He wore black Ray-Bans, and when he hit the end of the runway, he pulled them down a fraction of an inch, struck a pose, and looked out at the crowd with a half-smile on his face.

"Hey, sit down, I want to see the cute guy up there!" a girl behind them demanded.

Andie turned to her. "That guy?" She crooked her thumb at Pacey incredulously.

"Of course, that guy. Now sit down!"

She sat, too stunned to speak.

"I'm hallucinating, right?" Jen asked.

Joey laughed. "He really does look cute, you know?"

Andie put two fingers into her mouth and whistled at Pacey. He was at their side of the runway now, hitting another pose. His eyes lit on Andie. He grinned. Then winked. Then he sauntered off.

The girl behind Andie nudged her hard. "Hey, that guy winked at you!"

Dawson just shook his head. "I don't believe what I just saw."

A few minutes later, Pacey came out onto the runway again, this time in red flannel pajamas with sexy drawstring bottoms. The shirt was open, flapping insouciantly as he strutted down the runway. This time, when he posed near Andie, he put both of his hands over his heart and just looked at her, wide-eyed.

"That hot guy wants you bad!" the girl behind Andie yelped, clapping Andie so hard on the shoulder that she almost fell off her seat. "Lucky you!"

Dawson just kept shaking his head. "I still can't believe it."

The show ended when Sloan herself was carried out in the arms of the four male models, in a bridal-inspired white gown over a white and silver leather corset. She threw a bouquet of silver flowers into the crowd, and the show was over.

Within minutes, Pacey, clad in his own khakis and a bowling shirt, and still wearing his sunglasses, was pushing his way through the crowd to them. But he was stopped every few feet by some girl who told him how great he had been.

"It's the one and only Buffman!" Joey cheered when Pacey finally reached them.

Pacey held his palms up to them. "Please, please, no autographs." He lifted his glasses and looked at Andie. "You want me. Desperately. Admit it, and I might let you have your way with me."

"Do you have any idea how affected it is to wear sunglasses in a dark club?" Andie countered.

"Yes, I do," Pacey said solemnly. "I was going for that deeply affected effect."

"You weren't even surprised to see me, were you?" Andie realized.

Pacey grinned. "Joey told me she invited you to this thing. I just never told Joey I was in it. Surprised?"

"Major," Andie said. She folded her arms. "Did you and Sloan have a nice time?"

"This is where we discreetly remove ourselves from hearing distance," Dawson said to Joey and Jen. The three of them began to edge away.

"No, wait," Pacey called to them. "You can all hear this. Sloan did get me this gig. One of the models sprained his ankle or something, and she thought of me. Because I bodybuild."

"You look exactly the same, Pacey," Andie challenged.

"Hey, hey you," a cute brunette called to Pacey. "You were hot!"

"Thanks!" Pacey called back. He turned to Dawson. "You call yourself a friend? Why are you not videoing this for my personal archives?"

"It will live forever in our minds," Dawson assured him.

"It'll sure live on in mine," Andie said. "You really suck, Pacey, you know that? Pretending you stopped seeing Sloan just so you could get me here and rub my face in it—"

Pacey took off his sunglasses. "Wait, wait, is that what you think?"

Jen shrugged. "That's how it looks, Pacey."

"I did break it off with Sloan," Pacey insisted. "She's dating her astrologer now. She just thought that I'd make a good model. And much to my own shock, I did, actually."

Joey smiled slowly. "Yeah. You did."

"Oh, wow!"

The voice was familiar. It was Sloan, running over

to them. To Andie's shock, Sloan threw her arms around her.

"You're Andie, right? Pacey told me all about you. I'm so glad you guys are, like, back together." She kissed Pacey's cheek. "See ya, Pacey Buffman!"

"Exhibit one, for the defense. Mark it, and put it into evidence," Pacey said smugly.

Andie nodded reluctantly. "Okay, so maybe I was a bit hasty."

"I tell ya, this could be the start of big things for me," Pacey mused. "Today some little fashion bash in Roxbury. Tomorrow an exclusive with Calvin Klein. I can see it. I could become the next hot thing."

"Dream on, Pacey Buffman," Andie said.

Pacey reached for her hand. "I wasn't entirely . . . unappealing up there. Was I?"

"Not entirely," Andie mumbled, looking at the floor. "Let's face it. I can't compete with a girl like Sloan. That face, that body—" She raised her eyes.

"You don't need to compete," he said. "With anyone." And then he took her into his arms, and they danced together to the ballad Lenny Kravitz was singing through the sound system.

"Dance, Joey?" Dawson asked.

She looked around. "Where's Jen?"

"Some guy asked her to dance five minutes ago," Dawson told her. "You were so busy watching Pacey and Andie, you didn't notice."

"Jen was really nice to me, Dawson. She figured out how to get my photos taken off the Internet forever."

He nodded. Jen had already told him.

"And I'm not always so nice to her," Joey went on. "I should go find her—"

"I told you, she's dancing. You can say whatever you want to say to her later." He held his hands out to her, not really certain that she'd say yes to dancing with him.

And she didn't.

Instead, she just stepped into his embrace.

Dawson and Joey, she thought. She closed her eyes and, for once, let herself just feel instead of think. Dawson's arms were around her, her head rested against his chin, and the world was safe and wonderful, and dangerous, too, but in a safe and wonderful way.

"Once, I asked my father what made him fall in love with my mother," Dawson murmured to Joey as they danced. "He told me it was how she walked into a room, something like that, some purely physical thing. And now I look at them, Joey, so torn apart I don't know if they can ever be fixed. And I think—I know—that real love, lasting love, has to be so much more than that."

"You're hopeless, Dawson," Joey said. "A hopeless romantic. You're the only guy in America who believes that looks don't count."

"You mean would I . . . feel the way I feel about you if you weren't beautiful?" Dawson asked.

Joey made a face. "You don't think I'm beautiful, Dawson, so let's give that one a rest."

"You're right," he agreed.

Something in Joey's heart twisted painfully.

"I don't think you're beautiful," Dawson continued, "I *know* you're beautiful. And whether you're my girlfriend or my best friend, that doesn't change, Joey. You're beautiful when my eyes are closed. In my dreams. Eighty years from now. It won't matter."

"You don't know that."

"Yes, I do. And this time, Joey, I get the last word."

She was about to say: "This time, Dawson, I'll let you."

But she didn't.

Instead, she put her head against him, held him tight, and danced.

About the Author

C. J. Anders is a pseudonym for a well-known young adult fiction-writing couple.

Dawson's Creek

Trouble in Paradise
An ALL-NEW, ORIGINAL STORY
Featuring the characters of
Dawson's Creek

Here comes trouble...

To promote fall tourism, Capeside has a new slogan, "Fall in Love in Capeside," and a new weekend romance festival, including a kissing marathon. Pacey can't wait, but Andie's not interested. Then there's the contest for best romantic video that Dawson's dying to win, if only he could decide who should get the female lead.

Jen's visiting cousin Courtney might be just right for the role. She's not acting mean anymore. She's actually...nice. *Way* too nice, think Joey and Jen. And their instincts are right, because when Courtney teams up with Abby, watch out Capeside!

**Based on the hit television show
produced by Columbia TriStar Television**

Published by Pocket Books